Julie
McNamara

MRS PEPPERPOT'S
FIRST STORYBOOK

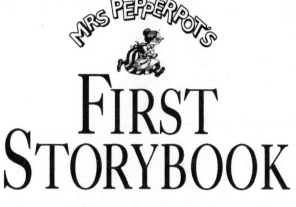

FIRST STORYBOOK

Alf Prøysen

Illustrated by
BJÖRN BERG

HUTCHINSON
London Sydney Auckland Johannesburg

This edition first published in 1998

1 3 5 7 9 10 8 6 4 2

Text © Alf Prøysen 1959, 1960, 1963, 1973
English translations © Hutchinson Children's Books 1959, 1960, 1963, 1973
Illustrations © Björn Berg 1959, 1960, 1963, 1973
Cover illustrations © Hilda Offen 1998

Alf Prøysen, Björn Berg and Hilda Offen have asserted their right under the
Copyright, Designs and Patents Act 1988, to be identified as the author
and illustrators of this work.

First published in the United Kingdom in 1998 by
Hutchinson Children's Books
Random House UK Limited
20 Vauxhall Bridge Road, London, SW1V 2SA

Random House Australia (Pty) Limited
20 Alfred Street, Milsons Point, Sydney
New South Wales 2061, Australia

Random House New Zealand Limited
18 Poland Road, Glenfield
Auckland 10, New Zealand

Random House South Africa (Pty) Limited
Endulini, 5A Jubilee Road, Parktown 2193, South Africa

Random House UK Limited Reg. No. 954009

A CIP catalogue record for this book is available from the British Library

ISBN: 0 09 176912 4

Printed and bound in Great Britain by
Mackays of Chatham PLC, Chatham, Kent

CONTENTS

Little old Mrs. Pepperpot

THERE was once an old woman who went to bed at night as old women usually do, and in the morning she woke up as old women usually do. But on this particular morning she found herself shrunk to the size of a pepper-pot, and old women don't usually do that. The odd thing was, her name really was Mrs. Pepperpot.

'Well, as I'm now the size of a pepperpot, I shall have to make the best of it,' she said to herself, for she had no one else to talk to; her husband was out in the fields and all her children were grown up and gone away.

Now she happened to have a great deal to do that day. First of all she had to clean the house, then there was all the washing which was lying in soak and waiting to be done, and lastly she had to make pancakes for supper.

'I must get out of bed somehow,' she thought, and, taking hold of a corner of the eiderdown, she started rolling herself up in it. She rolled and rolled until the eiderdown was like a huge sausage, which fell softly on the floor. Mrs. Pepperpot crawled out and she hadn't hurt herself a bit.

The first job was to clean the house, but that was quite easy; she just sat down in front of a mouse-hole and squeaked till the mouse came out.

'Clean the house from top to bottom,' she said, 'or I'll tell the cat about you.' So the mouse cleaned the house from top to bottom.

Mrs. Pepperpot called the cat: 'Puss! Puss! Lick out all the plates and dishes or I'll tell the dog about you.' And the cat licked all the plates and dishes clean.

Then the old woman called the dog. 'Listen, dog; you make the bed and open the window and I'll give you a bone as a reward.' So the dog did as he was told, and when he had finished he sat down on the front door-step and waved his tail so hard he made the step shine like a mirror.

'You'll have to get the bone yourself,' said Mrs. Pepperpot, 'I haven't time to wait on people.' She pointed to the window-sill where a large bone lay.

After this she wanted to start her washing. She had put it to soak in the brook, but the brook was almost dry. So she sat down and started muttering in a discontented sort of way:

'I have lived a long time, but in all my born days I never saw the brook so dry. If we don't have a shower soon, I expect everyone will die of thirst.' Over and over again she said it, all the time looking up at the sky.

At last the raincloud in the sky got so angry that it decided to drown the old woman altogether. But she crawled under a monk's-hood flower, where she stayed snug and warm while the rain poured down and rinsed her clothes clean in the brook.

Now the old woman started muttering again: 'I have lived a long time, but in all my born days I have never known such a feeble South Wind as we have had lately. I'm sure if the South Wind started blowing this minute it couldn't lift me off the ground, even though I am no bigger than a pepperpot.'

The South Wind heard this and instantly came tearing along, but Mrs. Pepperpot hid in an empty badger set, and from there she watched the South Wind blow all the clothes right up on to her clothes-line.

Again she started muttering: 'I have lived a long time, but in all my born days I have never seen the sun give so little heat in the middle of the summer. It seems to have lost all its power, that's a fact.'

When the sun heard this it turned scarlet with rage and sent down fiery rays to give the old woman sunstroke. But by this time she was safely back in her house, and was sailing about the sink in a saucer. Meanwhile the furious sun dried all the clothes on the line.

'Now for cooking the supper,' said Mrs. Pepperpot; 'my husband will be back in an hour and, by hook or by crook, thirty pancakes must be ready on the table.'

She had mixed the dough for the pancakes in a bowl the day before. Now she sat down beside the bowl and said: 'I have always been fond of you, bowl, and I've told all the neighbours that there's not a bowl like you any-where. I am sure, if you really wanted to, you could walk straight over to the cooking-stove and turn it on.'

And the bowl went straight over to the stove and turned it on.

Then Mrs. Pepperpot said: 'I'll never forget the day I bought my frying-pan. There were lots of pans in the shop, but I said: "If I can't have that pan hanging right over the shop assistant's head, I won't buy any pan at all. For that is the best pan in the whole world, and I'm sure if I were ever in trouble that pan could jump on to the stove by itself." '

And there and then the frying-pan jumped on to the stove. And when it was hot enough, the bowl tilted itself to let the dough run on to the pan.

Then the old woman said: 'I once read a fairy-tale about a pancake which could roll along the road. It was the stupidest story that ever I read. But I'm sure the pan-cake on the pan could easily turn a somersault in the air if it really wanted to.'

At this the pancake took a great leap from sheer pride and turned a somersault as Mrs. Pepperpot had said. Not only one pancake, but *all* the pancakes did this, and the bowl went on tilting and the pan went on frying until, before the hour was up, there were thirty pancakes on the dish.

Then Mr. Pepperpot came home. And, just as he opened the door, Mrs. Pepperpot turned back to her usual size. So they sat down and ate their supper.

And the old woman said nothing about having been as small as a pepperpot, because old women don't usually talk about such things.

Mrs. Pepperpot and the mechanical doll

IT WAS two days before Christmas. Mrs. Pepperpot hummed and sang as she trotted round her kitchen, she was so pleased to be finished with all her Christmas preparations. The pig had been killed, the sausages made, and now all she had to do was to brew herself a cup of coffee and sit down for a little rest.

'How lovely that Christmas is here,' she said, 'then everybody's happy—especially the children—that's the best of all; to see them happy and well.'

The old woman was almost like a child herself because of this knack she had of suddenly shrinking to the size of a pepperpot.

She was thinking about all this while she was making her coffee, and she had just poured it into the cup when there was a knock at the door.

'Come in,' she said, and in came a little girl who was oh! so pale and thin.

'Poor child! Wherever do you live—I'm sure I've never seen you before,' said Mrs. Pepperpot.

'I'm Hannah. I live in the little cottage at the edge of

the forest,' said the child, 'and I'm just going round to all the houses to ask if anybody has any old Christmas decorations left over from last year—glitter or paper-chains or glass balls or anything, you know. Have *you* got anything you don't need?'

'I expect so, Hannah,' answered Mrs. Pepperpot, and went up into the attic to fetch the cardboard box with all the decorations. She gave it to the little girl.

'How lovely! Can I really have all that?'

'You can,' said Mrs. Pepperpot, 'and you shall have something else as well. Tomorrow I will bring you a big doll.'

'I don't believe that,' said Hannah.

'Why not?'

'You haven't *got* a doll.'

'That's simple; I'll buy one,' said Mrs. Pepperpot. 'I'll bring it over tomorrow afternoon, but I must be home by six o'clock because it's Christmas Eve.'

'How wonderful if you can come tomorrow afternoon—I shall be all alone. Father and Mother both go out to work, you see, and they don't get back until the church bells have rung.'

So the little girl went home, and Mrs. Pepperpot went down to the toy-shop and bought a big doll. But when she woke up next morning there she was, once more, no bigger than a pepperpot.

'How provoking!' she said to herself. 'On this day of all days, when I have to take the doll to Hannah. Never mind! I expect I'll manage.'

After she had dressed she tried to pick up the doll, but it was much too heavy for her to lift.

'I'll have to go without it,' she thought, and opened the door to set off.

But oh dear! it had been snowing hard all night, and the little old woman soon sank deep in the snowdrifts. The cat was sitting in front of the house; when she saw something moving in the snow she thought it was a mouse and jumped on it.

'Hi, stop!' shouted Mrs. Pepperpot. 'Keep your claws to yourself! Can't you see it's just me shrunk again?'

'I beg your pardon,' said the cat, and started walking away.

'Wait a minute,' said Mrs. Pepperpot, 'to make up for your mistake you can give me a ride down to the main road.' The cat was quite willing, so she lay down and let the little old woman climb on her back. When they got to the main road the cat stopped. 'Can you hear anything?' asked Mrs. Pepperpot.

'Yes, I think it's the snow-plough,' said the cat, 'so we'll have to get out of the way, or we'll be buried in snow.'

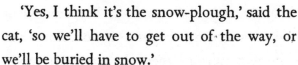

'I don't want to get out of the way,' said Mrs. Pepperpot, and she sat down in the middle of the road and waited till the snow-plough was right in front of her; then she jumped up and landed smack on the front tip of the plough.

There she sat, clinging on for dear life and enjoying herself hugely. 'Look at me, the little old woman, driving the snow-plough!' she laughed.

When the snow-plough had almost reached the door of Hannah's little cottage, she climbed on to the edge nearest the side of the road and, before you could say Jack Robinson, she had landed safely on the great mound of snow thrown up by the plough. From there she could walk right across Hannah's hedge and slide down the other side. She was shaking the snow off her clothes on the doorstep when Hannah came out and picked her up.

'Are you one of those mechanical dolls that you wind up?' asked Hannah.

'No,' said Mrs. Pepperpot, 'I am a woman who can wind myself up, thank you very much. Help me brush off all the snow and then let's go inside.'

'Are you perhaps the old woman who shrinks to the size of a pepperpot?'

'Of course I am, silly.'

'Where's the doll you were going to bring me?' asked Hannah when they got inside.

'I've got it at home. You'll have to go back with me and fetch it. It's too heavy for me.'

'Shouldn't you have something to eat, now that you've come to see me? Would you like a biscuit?' And the little girl held out a biscuit in the shape of a ring.

'Thank you very much,' said Mrs. Pepperpot and popped her head through the biscuit ring.

Oh, how the little girl laughed! 'I quite forgot you were so small,' she said; 'let me break it into little pieces so that you can eat it.' Then she fetched a thimble and filled it with fruit juice. 'Have a drink,' she said.

'Thank you,' said Mrs. Pepperpot.

After that they played a lot of good games; ride-a-cock-horse with Mrs. Pepperpot sitting on Hannah's knee, and hide-and-seek. But the little girl had an awful time trying to find Mrs. Pepperpot—she hid in such awkward places. When they had finished playing Hannah put on her coat and with Mrs. Pepperpot in her pocket she went off to fetch her beautiful big doll.

'Oh, thank you!' she exclaimed when she saw it. 'But do you know,' she added, 'I would really rather have *you* to play with all the time.'

'You can come and see me again if you like,' said Mrs. Pepperpot, 'I am often as small as a pepperpot, and then it's nice to have a little help around the house. And, of course, we can play games as well.'

So now the little girl often spends her time with Mrs. Pepperpot. She looks ever so much better, and they often talk about the day Mrs. Pepperpot arrived on the snow-plough, and about the doll she gave Hannah.

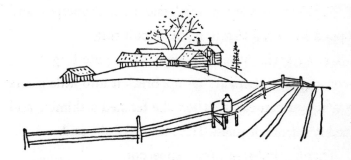

Mr. Pepperpot buys macaroni

'IT'S a very long time since we've had macaroni for supper,' said Mr. Pepperpot one day.

'Then you shall have it today, my love,' said his wife. 'But I shall have to go to the grocer for some. So first of all you'll have to find me.'

'Find you?' said Mr. Pepperpot. 'What sort of nonsense is that?' But when he looked round for her he couldn't see her anywhere. 'Don't be silly, wife,' he said; 'if you're hiding in the cupboard you must come out this minute. We're too big to play hide-and-seek.'

'*I'm* not too big, I'm just the right size for "hunt-the-pepperpot",' laughed Mrs. Pepperpot. 'Find me if you can!'

'I'm not going to charge round my own bedroom looking for my wife,' he said crossly.

'Now, now! I'll help you; I'll tell you when you're warm. Just now you're very cold.' For Mr. Pepperpot was peering out of the window, thinking she might have jumped out. As he searched round the room she called out 'Warm!', 'Colder!', 'Getting hotter!' until he was quite dizzy.

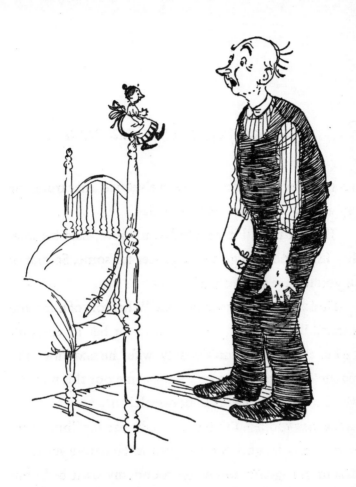

At last she shouted, 'You'll burn the top of your bald head if you don't look up!' And there she was, sitting on the bedpost, swinging her legs and laughing at him.

Her husband pulled a very long face when he saw her. 'This is a bad business—a very bad business,' he said, stroking her cheek with his little finger.

'I don't think it's a bad business,' said Mrs. Pepperpot.

'I shall have a terrible time. The whole town will laugh when they see I have a wife the size of a pepperpot.'

'Who cares?' she answered. 'That doesn't matter a bit. Now put me down on the floor so that I can get ready to go to the grocer and buy your macaroni.'

But her husband wouldn't hear of her going; he would go to the grocer himself.

'That'll be a lot of use!' she said. 'When you get home you'll have forgotten to buy the macaroni. I'm sure even if I wrote "macaroni" right across your forehead you'd bring back cinnamon and salt herrings instead.'

'But how are you going to walk all that way with those tiny legs?'

'Put me in your coat pocket; then I won't need to walk.'

There was no help for it, so Mr. Pepperpot put his wife in his pocket and set off for the shop.

Soon she started talking: "My goodness me, what a lot of strange things you have in your pocket—screws and nails, tobacco and matches—there's even a fish-hook! You'll have to take that out at once; I might get it caught in my skirt.'

'Don't talk so loud,' said her husband as he took out the fish-hook. 'We're going into the shop now.'

It was an old-fashioned village store where they sold everything from prunes to coffee cups. The grocer was particularly proud of the coffee cups and held one up for Mr. Pepperpot to see. This made his wife curious and she popped her head out of his pocket.

'You stay where you are!' whispered Mr. Pepperpot.

'I beg your pardon, did you say anything?' asked the grocer.

'No, no, I was just humming a little tune,' said Mr. Pepperpot. 'Tra-la-la!'

'What colour are the cups?' whispered his wife. And her husband sang:

'The cups are blue
With gold edge too,
But they cost too much
So that won't do!'

After that Mrs. Pepperpot kept quiet—but not for long. When her husband pulled out his tobacco tin she couldn't resist hanging on to the lid. Neither her husband nor anyone else in the shop noticed her slipping on to the counter and hiding behind a flour-bag. From there she darted silently across to the scales, crawled under them, past a pair of kippers wrapped in newspaper, and found herself next to the coffee cups.

'Aren't they pretty!' she whispered, and took a step backwards to get a better view. Whoops! She fell right into the macaroni drawer which had been left open. She hastily covered herself up with macaroni, but the grocer heard the scratching noise and quickly banged the drawer shut. You see, it did sometimes happen that mice got in the drawers, and that's not the sort of thing you want people to know about, so the grocer pretended nothing had happened and went on serving.

There was Mrs. Pepperpot all in the dark; she could hear the grocer serving her husband now. 'That's good,' she thought. 'When he orders macaroni I'll get my chance to slip into the bag with it.'

But it was just as she had feared; her husband forgot what he had come to buy. Mrs. Pepperpot shouted at the top of her voice, 'MACARONI!', but it was impossible to get him to hear.

'A quarter of a pound of coffee, please,' said her husband.

'Anything else?' asked the grocer.

'MACARONI!' shouted Mrs. Pepperpot.

'Two pounds of sugar,' said her husband.

'Anything more?'

'MACARONI!' shouted Mrs. Pepperpot.

But at last her husband remembered the macaroni of his own accord. The grocer hurriedly filled a bag. He thought he felt something move, but he didn't say a word.

'That's all, thank you,' said Mr. Pepperpot. When he got outside the door he was just about to make sure his

wife was still in his pocket when a van drew up and offered to give him a lift all the way home. Once there he took off his knapsack with all the shopping in it and put his hand in his pocket to lift out his wife.

The pocket was empty.

Now he was really frightened. First he thought she was teasing him, but when he had called three times and still no wife appeared, he put on his hat again and hurried back to the shop.

The grocer saw him coming. 'He's probably going to complain about the mouse in the macaroni,' he thought.

'Have you forgotten anything, Mr. Pepperpot?' he asked, and smiled as pleasantly as he could.

Mr. Pepperpot was looking all round. 'Yes,' he said.

'I would be very grateful, Mr. Pepperpot, if you would keep it to yourself about the mouse being in the macaroni. I'll let you have these fine blue coffee cups if you'll say no more about it.'

'Mouse?' Mr. Pepperpot looked puzzled.

'Shh!' said the grocer, and hurriedly started wrapping up the cups.

Then Mr. Pepperpot realized that the grocer had mistaken his wife for a mouse. So he took the cups and rushed home as fast as he could. By the time he got there he was in a sweat of fear that his wife might have been squeezed to death in the macaroni bag.

'Oh, my dear wife,' he muttered to himself. 'My poor darling wife. I'll never again be ashamed of you being the size of a pepperpot—as long as you're still alive!'

When he opened the door she was standing by the cooking-stove, dishing up the macaroni—as large as life; in fact, as large as you or I.

Queen of the Crows

DID you know that the woman who was as small as a pepperpot was queen of all the crows in the forest?

No, of course you didn't, because it was a secret between Mrs. Pepperpot and me until now. But now I'm going to tell you how it happened.

Outside the old woman's house there was a wooden fence and on it used to sit a large crow.

'I can't understand why that crow has to sit there staring in at the kitchen window all the time,' said Mr. Pepperpot.

'I can't imagine,' said Mrs. Pepperpot. 'Shoo! Get along with you!'

But the crow didn't move from the fence.

Then one day Mrs. Pepperpot had her shrinking turn again (I can't remember now what she was supposed to be doing that day, but she was very busy), and by the time she had clambered over the doorstep she was quite out of breath.

'Oh dear, it's certainly hard to be so small,' she puffed.

Suddenly there was a sound of flapping wings and the

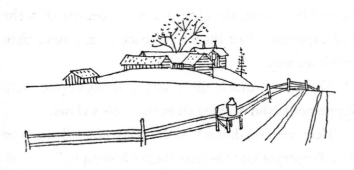

crow swooped down, picked up Mrs. Pepperpot by her skirt and flew up over the highest fir trees in the forest with her.

'What's the idea, may I ask? You wait till I'm back to my proper size and I'll beat you with my birch rod and chase you off for good!'

'Caw-caw! You're small enough now, at any rate,' said the crow; 'I've waited a long time for this. I saw you turn small once before, you see, so I thought it might happen again. And here we are, but only just in time. Today is the Crows' Festival and *I'm* to be Queen of the Crows!'

'If you're to be Queen of the Crows, you surely don't need to take an old woman like me along?'

'That's just where you're wrong,' said the crow, and flapped her wings; the old woman was heavier than she had expected. 'Wait till we get back to my nest, then you'll see why.'

'There's not much else I *can* do,' thought poor Mrs. Pepperpot as she dangled from the crow's claws.

'Here we are; home!' said the crow, and dropped Mrs. Pepperpot into the nest. 'Lucky it's empty.'

'It certainly is; I fell right on a spiky twig and grazed my shinbone.'

'Poor little thing!' said the crow. 'But look, I've made you a lovely bed of feathers and down. You'll find the down very snug and warm, and the feathers are just the thing when night falls and the wind begins to blow.'

'What do I want with feathers and down?'

'I want you to lie down and go to sleep,' said the crow. 'But first you must lend me your clothes. So please take off your head-scarf now, and your blouse and your skirt.

'The scarf I want you to tie round my neck, the skirt goes on one wing and the blouse on the other. Then I shall fly to the clearing in the forest where all the crows are meeting for the Festival. The finest-looking crow will be chosen queen, and that's going to be me! When I win I'll think of you. Caw-caw!'

'Well, if you think you'll be any better looking in my old clothes, you're welcome,' said Mrs. Pepperpot as she dressed up the crow.

'Hurry, hurry!' said the crow. 'There's another crow living over there in that fir tree on the hill. She'll be dropping in here on her way; we were going to the Festival together. But now that I'm all dressed up I'd rather go alone. Caw-caw-caw!' And off she flew.

Mrs. Pepperpot sat shivering in her petticoat, but then she thought of burrowing deep under the feathers and down as the crow had told her to do, and she found she was soon warm and cosy.

Suddenly the whole branch started swaying, and on the end perched a huge crow.

'Mary Crow, are you at home?' croaked the crow, sidling up and poking her big beak over the edge of the nest.

'Mary Crow has gone to the Festival,' said Mrs. Pepperpot.

'Then who are you, who are you?' asked the crow.

'I'm just an old woman shivering with cold, because Mary Crow has borrowed my clothes.'

'Caw-caw! Oh blow! She'll be the finest-looking crow at the Festival,' shrieked the crow as she threw herself into the air from the branch. 'But I'll have the scarf off her!'

Mrs. Pepperpot lay down to sleep again. Suddenly she rolled right over into the corner of the nest, the branch was shaking so much.

'That'll be another crow,' she thought, and quite right, it was; the biggest crow she had ever seen was swinging on the tip of the branch.

'Mary Crow, Mary Crow, have you seen Betty Crow?'

'I've seen both Mary Crow *and* Betty Crow,' said Mrs. Pepperpot.

'Who are you, who are you?' squawked the crow.

'I'm just an old woman shivering with cold because Mary Crow has borrowed my clothes.'

'Caw-caw! What a bore! Now Mary Crow will be the best-looking crow.'

'I'm not so sure about that,' said the old woman, 'because Betty Crow flew after Mary Crow and was going to have the scarf off her.'

'I'll take the skirt, I'll take the skirt!' croaked the biggest crow, and took off from the branch with such a bound that Mrs. Pepperpot had to hold on tight not to get thrown out of the nest.

In the clearing in the forest there were lots and lots of crows. They sat round in a circle and, one by one, they hopped into the middle to show themselves. Some of the crows could hop on one leg without touching the ground with their wings. Others had different kinds of tricks, and the crows sitting round had to choose the best one to be their queen.

At last there were only three crows left. They sat well away from each other, polishing their feathers and looking very fierce indeed. One had a scarf, the second had a skirt and the third had a blouse. So you can guess which crows *they* were. One of them was to be chosen queen.

'The crow with the scarf round her neck is the best,' said some of the crows, 'she looks most like a human being.'

'No, no; the crow with the skirt looks best!'

'Not at all! The crow with the blouse looks most dignified, and a queen should be dignified.'

Suddenly something fell with a bump to the ground; the jay had arrived right in the middle of the Festival with a strange-looking bird in its beak.

'Caw-caw! The jay has no business to be here!' croaked all the crows.

'I won't stay a minute,' said the jay. 'I've just brought you your queen!' and he flew off.

All the crows stared at the strange little raggedy bird in the middle of the ring. They could see it was covered in crow's feathers and down, but raggedy crows could not be allowed at the Festival.

'It's against the law!' said the biggest crow.

'Let's peck it, let's peck it!' said Mary Crow.

'Yes, let's hack it to pieces!' said Betty Crow.

'Yes, yes!' croaked all the crows. 'We can't have raggedy birds here!'

'Wait a minute!' said the raggedy bird, and climbed on to a tree-stump. 'I'll sing you a song.' And before they could stop it, it started singing 'Who Killed Cock Robin?' And it knew all the verses. The crows were delighted; they clapped and flapped their wings till the raggedy bird lost nearly all its feathers.

'D'you know any more? D'you know any more?' they croaked.

'I can dance the polka,' said the raggedy bird, and danced round the circle till they were all out of breath.

'You shall be our Queen!' they all shouted. 'Four Court Crows will carry you wherever you wish to go.'

'How wonderful!' laughed the Queen of the Crows. 'Then they must carry me to the house over there by the edge of the forest.'

'What would Your Majesty like to wear?'

'I would like to wear a skirt, a blouse and a head-scarf,' said the Queen.

Much later that night there was a knock at the cottage door. Mr. Pepperpot opened it, and there stood his wife.

'You're very late, wife,' he said. 'Where have you been?'

'I've been to a Festival,' she answered.

'But why are you covered in feathers?'

'You just go to bed and don't trouble yourself,' said Mrs. Pepperpot. She went over and stuck a feather in the corner of the window.

'Why do you do that?' asked her husband.

'For no reason at all.'

But she really did it because she had been chosen Queen of the Crows.

Mrs. Pepperpot at the bazaar

ONE day Mrs. Pepperpot was alone in her kitchen. At least, she was not *quite* alone, because Hannah, the little girl who had had the doll for Christmas, was there as well. She was busy scraping out a bowl and licking the spoon, for the old woman had been making gingerbread shapes.

There was a knock at the door. Mrs. Pepperpot said, 'Come in.' And in walked three very smart ladies.

'Good afternoon,' said the smart ladies. 'We are collecting prizes for the lottery at the school bazaar this evening. Do you think you have some little thing we could have? The money from the bazaar is for the boys' brass band—they need new instruments.'

'Oh, I'd like to help with that,' said Mrs. Pepperpot, for she dearly loved brass bands. 'Would a plate of gingerbread be any use?'

'Of course,' said the smart ladies, but they laughed behind her back. 'We could take it with us now if you have it ready,' they said. But Mrs. Pepperpot wanted to go to the bazaar herself, so she said she would bring the gingerbread.

So the three smart ladies went away and Mrs. Pepperpot was very proud and pleased that she was going to a bazaar.

Hannah was still scraping away at the bowl and licking the sweet mixture from the spoon.

'May I come with you?' she asked.

'Certainly, if your father and mother will let you.'

'I'm sure they will,' said the child, 'because Father has to work at the factory and Mother is at her sewing all day.'

'Be here at six o'clock then,' said Mrs. Pepperpot, and started making another batch of gingerbread shapes.

But when Hannah came back at six the old woman was not there. All the doors were open, so she went from room to room, calling her. When she got back to the kitchen she heard an odd noise coming from the table. The mixing bowl was upside down, so she lifted it carefully. And there underneath sat her friend who was now again as small as a pepperpot.

'Isn't this a nuisance?' said Mrs. Pepperpot. 'I was just cleaning out the bowl after putting the gingerbread in the oven when I suddenly started shrinking. Then the bowl turned over on me. Quick! Get the cakes out of the oven before they burn!'

But it was too late; the gingerbread was burnt to a cinder.

Mrs. Pepperpot sat down and cried, she was so disappointed. But she soon gave that up and started thinking instead. Suddenly she laughed out loud and said:

'Hannah! Put me under the tap and give me a good wash. We're going to the bazaar, you and I!'

'But you can't go to the bazaar like that!' said Hannah.

'Oh yes, I can,' said Mrs. Pepperpot, 'as long as you do what I say.'

Hannah promised, but Mrs. Pepperpot gave her some very queer orders. First she was to fetch a silk ribbon and tie it round the old woman so that it looked like a skirt. Then she was to fetch some tinsel from the Christmas decorations. This she had to wind round and round to make a silver bodice. And lastly she had to make a bonnet of gold foil.

'Now you must wrap me carefully in cellophane and put me in a cardboard box,' said Mrs. Pepperpot.

'Why?' asked Hannah.

'When I've promised them a prize for the bazaar they must have it,' said Mrs. Pepperpot, 'so I'm giving them myself. Just put me down on one of the tables and say you've brought a mechanical doll. Tell them you keep the key in your pocket and then pretend to wind me up so that people can see how clever I am.'

Hannah did as she was told, and when she got to the

bazaar and put the wonderful doll on the table, many people clapped their hands and crowded round to see.

'What a pretty doll!' they said. 'And what a lovely dress!'

'Look at her gold bonnet!'

Mrs. Pepperpot lay absolutely still in her cardboard box, but when she heard how everybody praised her, she winked at Hannah with one eye, and Hannah knew what she wanted. She lifted Mrs. Pepperpot very carefully out of the box and pretended to wind her up at the back with a key.

Everyone was watching her. But when Mrs. Pepperpot began walking across the table, picking her way through the prizes, there was great excitement.

'Look, the doll can walk!'

And when Mrs. Pepperpot began to dance they started shouting and yelling with delight, 'The doll is dancing!'

The three smart ladies who had been to see Mrs. Pepperpot earlier in the day sat in special seats and looked very grand. One of them had given six expensive coffee cups, the second an elegant table mat and the third a beautiful iced layer cake.

Mrs. Pepperpot decided to go over and speak to them, for she was afraid they had recognized her and thought it queer that she hadn't brought the gingerbread.

The three smart ladies were very pleased when the doll came walking across the table to them.

'Come to me!' said the one who had given the coffee cups, and stretched her hand out towards Mrs. Pepperpot, who walked on to it obediently.

'Let me hold her a little,' said the lady with the elegant table mat, and Mrs. Pepperpot went over to her hand.

'Now it's my turn,' said the lady with the iced cake.

'I'm sure they know it's me,' thought Mrs. Pepperpot, 'that's why they stare at me so hard and hold me on their hands.'

But then the lady with the cake said, 'Well, I must say, this is a much better prize than the gingerbread that the odd old woman offered us today.'

Now she should never have said that; Mrs. Pepperpot leaped straight out of her hand and landed PLOP! right in the middle of the beautiful iced layer cake. Then she got up and waded right through it. The cake lady screamed, but people were shouting with laughter by now.

'Take that doll away!' shrieked the second lady, but squish, squash! went Mrs. Pepperpot's sticky feet, right across her lovely table mat.

'Get that dreadful doll away!' cried the third lady. But it was too late; Mrs. Pepperpot was on the tray with

the expensive coffee cups, and began to dance a jig. Cups and saucers flew about and broke in little pieces.

What a-to-do! The conductor of the brass band had quite a job to quieten them all down. He announced that the winning numbers of the lottery would be given out.

'First prize will be the wonderful mechanical doll,' he said.

When Hannah heard that she was very frightened. What would happen if somebody won Mrs. Pepperpot, so that she couldn't go home to her husband? She tugged at Mrs. Pepperpot's skirt and whispered, 'Shall I put you in my pocket and creep away?'

'No,' said Mrs. Pepperpot.

'But think how awful it would be if someone won you and took you home.'

'What must be must be!' said Mrs. Pepperpot.

The conductor called out the winning number, '311!' Everyone looked at their tickets, but no one had number 311.

'That's a good thing!' sighed Hannah with relief. There would have to be another draw. But just then she remembered she had a ticket in her hand; it was number 311!

'Wait!' she cried, and showed her ticket. The conductor looked at it and saw it was the right one.

So Hannah was allowed to take Mrs. Pepperpot home.

Next day the old woman was her proper size again and Hannah only a little girl, and Mrs. Pepperpot said, 'You're my little girl, aren't you?'

'Yes,' said Hannah, 'and you're my very own Mrs. Pepperpot, because I won you at the bazaar yesterday.'

And that was the end of Mrs. Pepperpot's adventures for a very long time.

Mrs. Pepperpot and the Bilberries

THINGS were not very lively at Mrs. Pepperpot's house. Mr. Pepperpot was in a bad mood—he had been in it for days—and Mrs. Pepperpot simply didn't know how to get him out of it. She put flowers on the table and cooked him his favourite dish, fried bacon with macaroni cheese. But it was all no use; Mr. Pepperpot just went on moping.

'I don't know what's the matter with him,' sighed Mrs. Pepperpot, 'perhaps he's pining for pancakes.' So she made him a big pile of pancakes.

When her husband came in for dinner his face lit up at the sight of them, but as soon as he'd sat down and picked up his knife and fork to start eating, his face fell again; he was as glum as before.

'Ah well!' he said, staring up at the ceiling, 'I suppose it's too much to expect.'

'I've had enough of this!' cried Mrs. Pepperpot. 'You tell me what's wrong, or I'll *shrink*, so I will!' (You remember that Mrs. Pepperpot had a habit of shrinking to the size of a pepperpot, though not usually, I'm afraid, when she *wanted* to, but at the most inconvenient moments.) 'You have something on your mind, that's quite clear,' she went on. 'But you don't think of me, do you? Watching your face getting longer every day is no joke, I can tell you. Now even pancakes can't cheer you up.'

'Pancakes are all right,' nodded Mr. Pepperpot, 'but there's something else missing.'

'What could that be?' asked his wife.

'Couldn't we sometimes have a bit of bilberry jam with the pancakes, instead of just eating them plain?' And Mr. Pepperpot gave a great sigh.

At last she understood; it *was* a very long time since she had given him bilberry jam, and that was what the poor man had been missing.

'Well, if that's all you want, I'll go and pick some bilberries this very minute,' said Mrs. Pepperpot, and she snatched a bucket from a hook on the wall and rushed out of the door.

She walked rather fast because she was cross with her husband, and as she walked she talked to herself: 'I've got the silliest husband alive,' she muttered. 'I was a fool to marry him. In fact, there's only one bigger fool than me, and that's him. *Oh*, how stupid he is!'

In no time at all she reached the spot in the forest where the bilberries grew. She put her bucket under a bush and started picking into the cup she had in her apron pocket. Every time the cup was full she emptied it into the bucket. Cup after cup went in, until the bucket needed only one more cup to be quite full. But then, just as she had picked the last bilberry into the cup, lo and behold! She shrank to the size of a pepperpot.

'Now we're in a jam, that's certain, and I don't mean bilberry jam!' said the little old woman, who now had a tiny voice like a mouse. 'Still, I expect I can manage to get the cup as far as the bucket if I push and pull hard enough. After that we'll have to think again.'

So she crooked her arm through the handle and dragged the cup along. It was very hard at first, but then she came to an ant-path made of slippery pine-needles; here it was much easier, because the cup could slide along it. And all the time little ants and big ants kept scuttling to and fro beside her. She tried to talk to them.

'How d'you do, ants,' she said. 'Hard at work, I see. Yes, there's always plenty to do and that's a fact.' But the ants were far too busy to answer.

'Couldn't you stop for a minute and talk to me?' she asked. But they just hurried on. 'Well, I shall have to talk to myself; then I won't be disturbing anybody.' And she sat down with her back leaning against the cup.

As she sat there, she suddenly felt something breathe down her neck; she turned round, and saw a fox standing there waving his tail in a friendly sort of way.

'Hullo, Mr. Fox. Are you out for a stroll?' said Mrs. Pepperpot. 'Lucky you don't know my hens are . . . Oh dear! I nearly let my tongue run away with me!'

'Where did you say your hens were, Mrs. Pepperpot?' asked the fox in his silkiest voice.

'That would be telling, wouldn't it?' said Mrs. Pepperpot. 'But, as you see, I'm rather busy just now; I've got to get this cup of bilberries hauled over to the bucket somehow, so I haven't time to talk to you.'

'I'll carry the cup for you,' said the fox, as polite as could be. 'Then you can talk while we walk.'

'Thanks very much,' said Mrs. Pepperpot. 'As I was saying, my hens are . . . There now! I nearly said it again!'

The fox smiled encouragingly: 'Just go on talking, it doesn't matter what you say to *me*.'

'I'm not usually one to gossip, but somehow it seems so easy to talk about my hens being . . . Goodness, why don't I keep my mouth shut? Anyway, there's the bucket. So, if you would be so kind and set the cup down beside it I'll tell you where my hens are.'

'That's right, you tell me. Your hens will be quite safe with me.'

'They certainly will!' laughed Mrs. Pepperpot, 'for they're all away! They were broody, so I lent them to the neighbours to hatch out their eggs.'

Then the fox saw he had been tricked, and he was so ashamed he slunk away into the forest and hid himself.

'Ha, ha, ha! That was a fine trick you played on the fox!' said a voice quite close to Mrs. Pepperpot. She looked up and there stood a wolf towering over her.

'Well, if it isn't Mr. Wolf!' said Mrs. Pepperpot, swallowing hard to keep up her courage. 'The ve . . very person I need. You can help me tip this cup of bilberries into the bucket.'

'Oh no, you can't fool me like you did the fox,' said the wolf.

'I'm not trying to fool you at all,' said Mrs. Pepperpot; she had had a good idea and was no longer afraid. 'You'd better do as I say or I'll send for One-eye Threadless!'

The wolf laughed. 'I've heard many old wives' tales but I've never heard that one before!'

'It's not an old wives' tale,' said Mrs. Pepperpot indignantly, 'and I'm not just an old wife; I'm Mrs. Pepperpot who can shrink and grow again all in a flash. One-eye Threadless is my servant.'

'Ha, ha! I'd like to see that servant of yours!' laughed the wolf.

'Very well; stick your nose into my apron pocket here and you'll meet him,' said Mrs. Pepperpot. So the wolf put his nose in her apron pocket and pricked it very severely on a needle she kept there.

'Ow, ow!' he shouted and started running towards the forest. But Mrs. Pepperpot called him back at once: 'Come here! You haven't done your job yet; empty that cup into that bucket, and don't you dare spill a single berry, or I'll send for One-eye Threadless to prick you again!'

The wolf didn't dare disobey her, but as soon as he had emptied the cup into the bucket he ran like the fox to the forest to hide.

Mrs. Pepperpot had a good laugh as she watched him go, but then she heard something rustle near the bucket. This time it was the big brown bear himself.

'Dear me! What an honour!' said Mrs. Pepperpot in a shaky voice, and she curtsied so low she nearly disappeared in the bushes. 'Has the fine weather tempted Your Majesty out for a walk?'

'Yes,' growled the big brown bear and went on sniffing at the bucket.

'How very fortunate for me! As Your Majesty can see, I've picked a whole bucket of berries, but it's not very safe for a little old woman like myself to walk in the forest alone. Could I ask Your Majesty to carry the bucket out to the road for me?'

'I don't know about that,' said the bear. 'I like bilberries myself.'

'Yes, of course, but you're not like the rest of them,

Your Majesty; you wouldn't rob a poor little old woman like me!'

'Bilberries; that's what I want!' said the bear, and put his head down to start eating.

In a flash Mrs. Pepperpot had jumped on his neck and started tickling him behind his ears.

'What are you doing?' asked the bear.

'I'm just tickling your ears for you,' answered Mrs. Pepperpot. 'Doesn't it feel good?'

'Good? It's almost better than eating the berries!' said the bear.

'Well, if Your Majesty would be so kind as to carry the bucket, I could be tickling Your Majesty's ears all the way,' said the artful Mrs. Pepperpot.

'Oh, very well then,' grumbled the bear.

When they reached the road the bear put the bucket down very carefully on a flat stone.

'Many, many thanks, Your Majesty,' said Mrs. Pepperpot as she made another deep curtsey.

'Thank *you*,' said the bear, and shuffled off into the forest.

When the bear had gone Mrs. Pepperpot became her usual size again, so she picked up her bucket and hurried homeward.

'It's really not very difficult to look after yourself, even when you're only the size of a pepperpot,' she told herself. 'As long as you know how to tackle the people you meet. Cunning people must be tricked, cowardly ones must be frightened, and the big, strong ones must have their ears tickled.'

As for bad-tempered husbands, the only thing to do with *them* is to give them bilberry jam with their pancakes.

Mrs. Pepperpot minds the baby

Now I'll tell you what happened the day Mrs. Pepperpot was asked to mind the baby.

It was early in the morning. Mrs. Pepperpot had sent her husband off to work. In the usual way wives do, she had made the coffee and the sandwiches for his lunch, and had stood by the window and waved till he was out of sight. Then, just like other wives, she had gone back to bed to have a little extra shut-eye, leaving all her housework for later.

She had been sleeping a couple of hours when there was a knock at the door. She looked at the clock. 'Good heavens!' she cried, 'have I slept so long?' She pulled her clothes on very quickly and ran to open the door.

In the porch stood a lady with a little boy on her arm.

'Forgive me for knocking,' said the lady.

'You're welcome,' said Mrs. Pepperpot.

'You see,' said the lady, 'I'm staying with my aunt near here with my little boy, and today we simply *have* to go shopping in the town. I can't take Roger and there's no one in the house to look after him.'

'Oh, that's all right!' said Mrs. Pepperpot. 'I'll look after your little boy.' (To herself she thought: 'However will I manage with all that work and me oversleeping like that. Ah well, I shall have to do both at the same time.') Then she said out loud: 'Roger, come to Mrs. Pepperpot? That's right!' And she took the baby from the lady.

'You don't need to give him a meal,' said the lady. 'I've brought some apples he can have when he starts sucking his fingers.'

'Very well,' said Mrs. Pepperpot, and put the apples in a dish on the sideboard.

The lady said goodbye and Mrs. Pepperpot set the baby down on the rug in the sitting-room. Then she went out into the kitchen to fetch her broom to start sweeping up. At that very moment she *shrank*!

'Oh dear! Oh dear! Whatever shall I do?' she wailed, for of course now she was much smaller than the baby. She gave up any idea of cleaning the house; when her husband came home she would have to tell him that she had had a headache.

'I must go and see what that little fellow is doing,' she thought, as she climbed over the doorstep into the sitting-room. Not a moment too soon! For Roger had crawled right across the floor and was just about to pull the tablecloth off the table together with a pot of jam, a loaf of bread, and a big jug of coffee!

Mrs. Pepperpot lost no time. She knew it was too far for her to get to the table, so she pushed over a large silver cup which was standing on the floor, waiting to be polished. Her husband had won it in a skiing competition years ago when he was young.

The cup made a fine booming noise as it fell; the baby turned round and started crawling towards it.

'That's right,' said Mrs. Pepperpot, 'you play with that; at least you can't break it.'

But Roger wasn't after the silver cup. Gurgling: 'Ha' dolly! Ha' dolly!' he made a bee-line for Mrs. Pepperpot, and before she could get away, he had grabbed her by the waist! He jogged her up and down and every time Mrs. Pepperpot kicked and wriggled to get free, he laughed. ''Ickle, 'ickle!' he shouted, for she was tickling his hand with her feet.

'Let go! Let go!' yelled Mrs. Pepperpot. But Roger was used to his father shouting 'Let's go!' when he threw him up in the air and caught him again. So Roger shouted 'Leggo! Leggo!' and threw the little old woman up in the air with all the strength of his short arms. Mrs. Pepperpot went up and up—nearly to the ceiling! Luckily she landed on the sofa, but she bounced several times before she could stop.

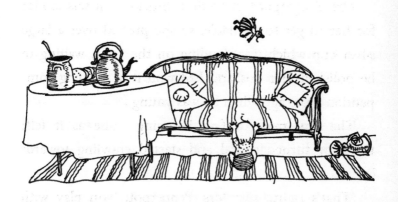

'Talk of flying through the air with the greatest of ease!' she gasped. 'If that had happened to me in my normal size I'd most likely have broken every bone in my body. Ah well, I'd better see what my little friend is up to now.'

She soon found out. Roger had got hold of a match-box and was trying to strike a match. Luckily he was using the wrong side of the box, but Mrs. Pepperpot had to think very quickly indeed.

'Youngsters like to copy everything you do, so I'll take this nut and throw it at him. Then he'll throw it at me—I hope.'

She had found the nut in the sofa and now she was in such a hurry to throw it she forgot to aim properly. But it was a lucky shot and it hit Roger just behind the ear, making him turn round. 'What else can I throw?' wondered Mrs. Pepperpot, but there was no need, because the baby had seen her; he dropped the match-box and started crawling towards the sofa.

'Ha' dolly! Ha' dolly!' he gurgled delightedly. And now they started a very funny game of hide-and-seek— at least it was fun for Roger, but not quite so amusing for poor little old Mrs. Pepperpot who had to hide behind the cushions to get away from him. In the end she managed to climb on to the sideboard where she kept a precious geranium in a pot.

'Aha, you can't catch me now!' she said, feeling much safer.

But at that moment the baby decided to go back to the match-box. 'No, no, no!' shouted Mrs. Pepperpot. Roger took no notice. So, when she saw he was trying to strike another match, she put her back against the flowerpot and gave it a push so that it fell to the floor with a crash.

Roger immediately left the match-box for this new and interesting mess of earth and bits of broken flowerpot. He buried both his hands in it and started putting it in his mouth, gurgling, 'Nice din-din!'

'No, no, no!' shouted Mrs. Pepperpot once more. 'Oh, whatever shall I do?' Her eye caught the apples left by Roger's mother. They were right beside her on the dish. One after the other she rolled them over the edge of the dish on to the floor. Roger watched them roll, then he decided to chase them, forgetting his lovely meal of earth and broken flowerpot. Soon the apples were all over the floor and the baby was crawling happily from one to the other.

There was a knock on the door.

'Come in,' said Mrs. Pepperpot.

Roger's mother opened the door and came in, and there was Mrs. Pepperpot as large as life, carrying a dustpan full of earth and broken bits in one hand and her broom in the other.

'Has he been naughty?' asked the lady.

'As good as gold,' said Mrs. Pepperpot. 'We've had a high old time together, haven't we, Roger?' And she handed him back to his mother.

'I'll have to take you home now, precious,' said the lady.

But the little fellow began to cry. 'Ha' dolly! Ha' dolly!' he sobbed.

'Have *dolly*?' said his mother. 'But you didn't bring a dolly—you don't even have one at home.' She turned to Mrs. Pepperpot. 'I don't know what he means.'

'Oh, children say so many things grown-ups don't understand,' said Mrs. Pepperpot, and waved goodbye to Roger and his mother.

Then she set about cleaning up her house.

Mrs. Pepperpot's penny watchman

STRANGE things had been happening in Mrs. Pepperpot's house. It all began when a little girl came to the door selling penny raffle tickets for a tablecloth. Mrs. Pepperpot hunted high and low until she found a penny; it was a nice shiny one, because someone had been polishing it. But just as she was writing her name on the ticket, the penny dropped on the floor and rolled into a crack by the trapdoor to the cellar.

'Bang goes my fortune,' said Mrs. Pepperpot, as she watched it disappear. 'Now I won't be able to buy a raffle ticket after all. But I can't let you go without giving you anything; what about a nice home-made short-cake?' And she stood on a stool to reach the cake-tin.

It was empty. Mrs. Pepperpot turned the tin almost inside out, but there was no sign of any short-cake.

'I can't understand it,' she said. 'I baked two whole rounds of short-cake on Friday. Today it's only Monday, and the tin is empty. Very mysterious. But I've got something you might like even better, little girl.' So

saying, Mrs. Pepperpot opened the trapdoor to the cellar
and went down the steps to fetch the big jar of bramble
jelly she had left over from the summer.

But what a sight met her eyes!

'Goodness Gracious and Glory Be!' she exclaimed,
for the big jar of bramble jelly was lying smashed under
the shelf with the jelly gently oozing out over the floor.
From the sticky mess a little trail of mouse footprints
ran across to the chimney.

There was nothing for it—Mrs. Pepperpot had to go
up to the little girl and tell her she couldn't even have
bramble jelly. But the little girl said it didn't matter a bit
and politely curtsied before going on to the next house.

Mrs. Pepperpot took a mouse-trap and went down the cellar steps again. She baited it with cheese and set it very carefully on the floor. When it was done she turned to go upstairs again, but the hem of her skirt brushed against it, and SNAP! went the trap, with a corner of her skirt caught in it. That was bad enough, but then, if you please, she shrank again!

'Now I really *am* stuck!' she told herself, and she certainly was; she couldn't move an inch. After she had sat there a while she saw a young mouse peeping over the edge of an empty flowerpot.

'You're quite safe to come out,' said Mrs. Pepperpot. 'I'm too well tethered to do you any harm at the moment.'

But the little mouse darted off to an empty cardboard box and then two little mice popped their noses over the edge.

'One and one makes two,' said Mrs. Pepperpot. 'I learned that at school, and I wouldn't be a bit surprised if you fetched a third one—for one and two make three!'

She was right. The two little mice darted off together and stayed away quite a long time while she sat and waited. Suddenly she heard a tinny little sound. Ping! Ping! And a big mouse came walking towards her on his hind legs, banging a shiny gong with a little steel pin. The shiny gong was Mrs. Pepperpot's lost penny!

The big mouse bowed low. 'Queen of the House, I greet you!' The little mice were peeping out from behind him.

'Thank goodness for that!' said Mrs. Pepperpot. 'For a moment I thought you might be coming to gobble me up—you're so much bigger than I am!'

'We're not in the habit of gobbling up queens,' said the large mouse. 'I just wanted to tell you, you have a thief in your house.'

Mrs. Pepperpot snorted. 'Thief indeed! Of course I have; you and all the other mice are the thieves in my house. Whose penny is it you're using for a gong, may I ask?'

'Oh, is that what it is? A penny?' said the big mouse. 'Well, it rolled through a crack in the floor, you see, so I thought I could use it to scare away the thief and to show I'm the watchman in this house. You really do need a watchman, Queen of the House, to keep an eye on things for you.'

'What nonsense!' said Mrs. Pepperpot. She tried to stand up, but it was rather difficult with her dress caught in the trap and she herself so tiny.

'Take it easy, Queen of the House,' said the big mouse. 'Let my son here tell you what he has seen.'

Timidly, one of the little mice came forward and told how he had climbed up the chimney one day and peeped through a hole into the kitchen. There he had seen a terrible monster who was eating up all the cake in the tin.

Then the other little mouse chirped in to tell how he had been playing hide-and-seek behind a jam-jar on the shelf when the monster had put out a huge hand and taken the jar away. But he had been so scared when he saw the little mouse that he had dropped the jar on the floor, and all the bramble jelly came pouring out.

Suddenly they heard Tramp! Tramp! Tramp! up above; the sound of huge boots walking about.

'That's the monster!' said one of the little mice.

'Yes, that's him all right!' said the other little mouse.

'Is it, indeed!' said Mrs. Pepperpot. 'If only I could get out of this trap, I should very much like to go and have a look at this monster.'

'We'll help you,' said all the mice, and they set to work to free Mrs. Pepperpot from the trap in the way only mice know how; they gnawed through her skirt, leaving a piece stuck in the spring.

'Now you must hurry up to the kitchen to see the monster,' they said.

'But how am I to get there?' asked Mrs. Pepperpot.

'Up through the chimney on our special rope; we'll pull you up.'

And that's what they did. They hoisted Mrs. Pepperpot higher and higher inside the chimney, until she could see a chink of light.

'That's the crack into the kitchen,' the big mouse told her from below.

She called down to him: 'Thank you Mr. Watchman, thank you for your help, and keep a sharp look-out!'

Then she climbed through the hole in the wall. As soon as she set foot on the floor she grew to her normal size. Standing in front of the stove, she put her hands on her hips and said, 'So it's you, husband, is it, who's been eating all my short-cake and stealing the bramble jelly in the cellar?'

Mr. Pepperpot looked dumbfounded: 'How did you know that?' he said.

'Because I have a watchman now, I have paid him a penny,' said Mrs. Pepperpot.

The bad luck story

IF YOU take the road past Mrs. Pepperpot's house and turn to the right, then to the left and carry straight on, you will come to a cottage.

In this cottage lived an old woman they called 'Mrs. Calamity', because she believed in omens and always expected the worst to happen. Another curious thing about her was that she had the habit of stealing cuttings from pot-plants in other people's houses. Not that this in itself was very serious, only sometimes the flowers died after she had been cutting them about. But Mrs. Calamity had the idea that stolen plants thrive much better than any you got as a present, which is just one of those old wives' tales.

One day she visited little old Mrs. Pepperpot. She sat on the edge of a chair very politely and talked about this and that, but all the time she was looking round at all the plants in Mrs. Pepperpot's window-sill.

'That's right; have a good look,' thought Mrs. Pepperpot to herself. 'I know what you're after; you want to take cuttings of my best geranium. But we'll see about that, my fine lady!'

Unfortunately, there was a knock at the door just at that moment, and Mrs. Pepperpot had to leave her visitor alone while she went to answer it.

A man stood there. 'Anyone called Cuthbertson live here?' he asked.

'Cuthbertson? There's never been anyone of that name in this house, as far as I know,' said Mrs. Pepperpot. 'You'd better ask at the post-office. Excuse me, I'm busy just now.' And she turned to shut the door.

Too late! For at that moment Mrs. Pepperpot shrank again!

She stretched her little neck as much as she could to look over the doorstep into the sitting-room. Sure enough! There was Mrs. Calamity ferreting about in Mrs. Pepperpot's flowerpots.

'I have a feeling you're going to regret that, Madam Thief,' thought Mrs. Pepperpot as she swung herself over the step into the yard. There she found a little wagtail pecking about, looking for something to eat.

'Hullo, little wagtail,' she said. 'If you'll help *me*, then I'll help *you*. You can have all the crumbs you want if you'll just go over to the front doorstep and stand quite still, facing the door.'

'That's easily done,' said the wagtail, and hopped across the yard.

No doubt Mrs. Calamity was wondering what had happened to the lady of the house. She came to the door and looked out, holding her hand carefully over her apron pocket where she had hidden the geranium cutting.

Then she caught sight of the wagtail on the step. 'Oh Calamity!' she wailed. 'I've looked a wagtail straight in the face and now I shall have bad luck for a year.'

And, clutching her apron pocket, she hurried away from the house.

But over her head the wagtail was following her, flying with Mrs. Pepperpot on its back. As she clung with her arms round the bird's neck, she said: 'D'you know where we could find a black cat?'

'A black cat?' answered the wagtail. 'I should think I do! The horrible creature was lying in wait for me down by the bend in the road. She's probably still there. So don't ask me to land anywhere near her.'

'Don't worry!' said Mrs. Pepperpot. 'I want you to put me down on the *opposite* side of the road—I have a little plan.'

So the wagtail did as she asked and flew out of harm's way as fast as it could go.

Mrs. Pepperpot crouched down in the long grass; she could see the cat's tail waving to and fro in the ditch

on the other side of the road. Soon she heard the clump, clump, clump of Mrs. Calamity's boots as she walked down the road.

Just as she came past where Mrs. Pepperpot was

hiding, Mrs. Pepperpot made the noise of a wagtail calling. The black cat heard it and, like a streak of lightning, shot across the road, right in front of Mrs. Calamity.

Mrs. Calamity stood stock-still with fright. 'A black cat!' she screamed. 'That means *three* years' bad luck!

Oh Calamity, what shall I do?' She was so alarmed she didn't dare go on; instead, she took the path through the wood to her house.

Meanwhile the cat was going in the same direction, for by now Mrs. Pepperpot was riding on her back. 'Have you seen any magpies about?' she asked the cat.

'I should think I have!' said the cat. 'There's a pair of them in that birch-tree over there; they tease me and pull my tail whenever they get the chance. Look! They're waiting for me now!'

'Then you can drop me here,' said Mrs. Pepperpot. 'Come and see me tomorrow and I'll give you a bowl of cream.'

The cat did as she asked, and a moment later Mrs. Pepperpot was talking to the magpies in the birch-tree.

'Good afternoon,' she said. 'I wonder if you would have such a thing as a key-ring in your nest?'

'Oh no,' said the magpies, 'we don't have key-rings, we only collect broken-mirror bits.'

'The best is good enough,' replied Mrs. Pepperpot. 'I want you to put some nice-looking bits on Mrs. Calamity's doorstep. If you can do that for me, I'll keep the curly tail for you when we kill the pig at Christmas.'

The magpies didn't need to be told twice. A little heap of broken-mirror bits were on Mrs. Calamity's doorstep before you could say Jack Robinson.

When she arrived and saw what was waiting for her Mrs. Calamity sat down and cried.

'Oh, misery me! Oh Calamity! A broken mirror will give me *seven* years' bad luck!'

But by now Mrs. Pepperpot had grown to her proper size again; quietly she came round the corner, and her voice was quite gentle when she spoke.

'Now, now, Mrs. Calamity,' she said, 'you mustn't sit here crying.'

'Oh, Mrs. Pepperpot! It's nothing but bad luck for me from beginning to end.' She sniffed, and she told Mrs. Pepperpot about the wagtail that had faced her, the cat that had jumped across her path and now the broken mirror. When she'd finished she fished for a handkerchief in her apron pocket.

Out fell the geranium cutting!

Mrs. Calamity picked it up and handed it to Mrs. Pepperpot. 'There—take it! I stole it from your house. Now you'd better have it back, for I shall never need geraniums or anything else in this world, I don't suppose!'

'Don't be silly,' said Mrs. Pepperpot. 'Let's forget about all this nonsense, shall we? I'm going to *give* you the cutting as a present. You plant it, and I'm sure you'll find that it'll grow into the finest flower you ever had.'

She was right. The tiny cutting grew into a huge geranium with bright red blooms, and that in spite of the fact that Mrs. Calamity not only thanked Mrs. Pepperpot, but shook hands as well, which is the worst thing you can do if you believe in bad omens.

But from then on she changed her ideas, and people no longer called her Mrs. Calamity, but plain Mrs. Brown instead.

Mrs. Pepperpot and the moose

It was winter-time, and Mrs. Pepperpot was having trouble getting water. The tap in her kitchen ran slower and slower, until one day it just dripped and then stopped altogether. The well was empty.

'Ah, well,' thought Mrs. Pepperpot, 'it won't be the first time I've had this kind of trouble, and it won't be the last. But with two strong arms and a good sound bucket, not to mention the lucky chance that there's another well down by the forest fence, we'll soon fix that.'

So she put on her husband's old winter coat and a pair of thick gloves and fetched a pick-axe from the wood-shed. Then she trudged through the snow down the hill, to where there was a dip by the forest fence. She swept the snow away and started breaking a hole in the ice with the pick-axe. Chips of ice flew everywhere as Mrs. Pepperpot hacked away, not looking to left or right. She made such a noise that she never heard the sound of breaking twigs, nor the snorting that was coming from the other side of the fence.

But there he was; a huge moose with great big antlers, not moving at all, but staring angrily at Mrs. Pepperpot. Suddenly he gave a very loud snort and leaped over the fence, butting Mrs. Pepperpot from behind, so that she went head-first into a pile of snow!

'What the dickens!' cried Mrs. Pepperpot as she scrambled to her feet. But by that time the moose was back on the other side of the fence. When she saw what

it was that had pushed her over, Mrs. Pepperpot lost no time in scrambling up the hill and into her house, locking the door behind her. Then she peeped out of the kitchen window to see if the moose was still there. He was.

'You wait, you great big brute!' said Mrs. Pepperpot. 'I'll give you a fright you won't forget!'

She put on a black rain-cape and a battered old hat, and in her hand she carried a big stick. Then she crept out of the door and hid round the corner of the house.

The moose was quietly nibbling the bark off the trees and seemed to be taking no notice of her.

Suddenly she stormed down the hill, shouting, 'Woollah, Woollah, Woollah!' like a Red Indian, the black rain-cape flapping round her and the stick waving in the air. The moose *should* have been frightened, but he just took one look at the whirling thing coming towards him, leaped the fence and headed straight for it!

Poor Mrs. Pepperpot! All she could do was to rush back indoors again as fast as she knew how.

'Now what shall I do?' she wondered. 'I must have water to cook my potatoes and do my washing-up, and a little cup of coffee wouldn't come amiss after all this excitement. Perhaps if I were to put on my old man's trousers and take his gun out . . . I could pretend to aim it; that might scare him off.'

So she put on the trousers and took out the gun; but this was the silliest idea she had had yet, because, before she was half-way down the hill, that moose came pounding towards her on his great long legs. She never had time to point the gun. Worse still, she dropped it in her efforts to keep the trousers up and run back to the house at the same time. When the moose saw her disappear indoors, he turned and stalked down the hill again, but this time he didn't jump back over the fence, but stayed by the well, as if he were guarding it.

'Ah well,' said Mrs. Pepperpot, 'I suppose I shall have to fill the bucket with snow and melt it to get the water I need. That moose is clearly not afraid of anything.'

So she took her bucket and went outside. But just as she was bending down to scoop up the snow, she turned small! But this time the magic worked quicker than usual, and somehow she managed to tumble into the bucket which was lying on its side. The bucket started to roll down the hill; faster and faster it went, and poor Mrs. Pepperpot was seeing stars as she bumped round and round inside.

Just above the dip near the well a little mound jutted out, and here the bucket made a leap into space. 'This is the end of me!' thought Mrs. Pepperpot. She waited for the bump, but it didn't come! Instead the bucket seemed to be floating through the air, over the

fence and right into the forest. If she had had time to think, Mrs. Pepperpot would have known that the moose had somehow caught the bucket on one of his antlers, but it is not so easy to think when you're swinging between heaven and earth.

At last the bucket got stuck on a branch and the moose thundered on through the undergrowth. Mrs. Pepperpot lay there panting, trying to get her breath back. She had no idea where she was. But then she heard: 'Chuck, chuck! Chuck, chuck!'—the chattering of **a** squirrel as he ran down the tree-trunk over her head.

'Hullo!' said the squirrel, 'if it isn't Mrs. Pepperpot! Out for a walk, or something?'

'Not exactly a *walk*,' said Mrs. Pepperpot, 'but I've had a free ride, though I don't know who gave it to me.'

'That was the King of the Moose,' said the squirrel. 'I saw him gallop past with a wild look in his eyes. It's the first time I have ever seen him afraid, I can tell you that. He is so stupid and so stuck-up you wouldn't believe it. All he thinks of is fighting; he goes for anything and anybody—the bigger the better. But you seem to have given him the fright of his life.'

'I'm glad I managed it in the end,' said Mrs. Pepperpot, 'and now I'd be gladder still if I knew how to get myself home.'

But she needn't have worried, because at that moment she felt herself grow large again, and the next thing she knew she had broken the branch and was lying on the ground. She picked herself and her bucket up and started walking home. But when she got to the fence she took a turn down to the well to fill the bucket.

When she stood up she looked back towards the forest, and there, sure enough, stood the moose, blinking at her. But Mrs. Pepperpot was no longer afraid of him. All she had to do was to rattle that bucket a little, and the big creature shook his head and disappeared silently into the forest.

From that day on Mrs. Pepperpot had no trouble fetching water from the well by the forest fence.

Mrs. Pepperpot finds a hidden treasure

IT WAS a fine sunny day in January, and Mrs. Pepperpot was peeling potatoes at the kitchen sink.

'Miaow!' said the cat; she was lying in front of the stove.

'Miaow yourself!' answered Mrs. Pepperpot.

'Miaow!' said the cat again.

Mrs. Pepperpot suddenly remembered an old, old rhyme she learned when she was a child. It went like this:

> The cat sat by the fire,
> Her aches and pains were dire,
> Such throbbing in my head,
> She cried; I'll soon be dead!

'Poor Pussy! Are your aches and pains so bad? Does your head throb?' she said, and smiled down at the cat.

But the cat only looked at her.

Mrs. Pepperpot stopped peeling potatoes, wiped her hands and knelt down beside the cat. 'There's something you want to tell me, isn't there, Pussy? It's too bad I can't understand you except when I'm little, but it's not my fault.' She stroked the cat, but Pussy didn't purr, just went on looking at her.

'Well, I can't spend all day being sorry for you, my girl, I've got a husband to feed,' said Mrs. Pepperpot, and went back to the potatoes in the sink. When they were ready she put them in a saucepan of cold water on the stove, not forgetting a good pinch of salt. After that she laid the table, for her husband had to have his dinner sharp at one o'clock and it was now half past twelve.

Pussy was at the door now. 'Miaow!' she said, scratching at it.

'You want to get out, do you?' said Mrs. Pepperpot, and opened the door. She followed the cat out, because she had noticed that her broom had fallen over in the snow. The door closed behind her.

And at that moment she shrank to her pepperpot size!

'About time too!' said the cat. 'I've been waiting for days for this to happen. Now don't let's waste any more time; jump on my back! We're setting off at once.'

Mrs. Pepperpot didn't stop to ask where they were going; she climbed on Pussy's back. 'Hold on tight!' said Pussy, and bounded off down the little bank at the back of the house past Mrs. Pepperpot's rubbish-heap.

'We're coming to the first hindrance,' said Pussy; 'just sit tight and don't say a word!' All Mrs. Pepperpot could see was a single birch-tree with a couple of magpies on it. True, the birds seemed as big as eagles to her now and the tree was like a mountain. But when the magpies started screeching she knew what the cat meant.

'There's the cat! There's the cat!' they screamed. 'Let's nip her tail! Let's pull her whiskers!' And they swooped down, skimming so close over Mrs. Pepperpot's head she was nearly blown off the cat's back. But the cat took no notice at all, just kept steadily on down the hill, and the magpies soon tired of the game.

'That's that!' said the cat. 'The next thing we have to watch out for is being hit by snowballs. We have to cross the boys' playground now, so if any of them start aiming at you, duck behind my ears and hang on!'

Mrs. Pepperpot looked at the boys; she knew them all, she had often given them sweets and biscuits. '*They* can't be dangerous,' she said to herself.

But then she heard one of them say: 'There comes that stupid cat; let's see who can hit it first! Come on,

'So far, so good,' she said, 'but now comes the worst bit, because this is dog land, and we don't want to get caught. So keep your eyes skinned!'

The fence divided Mrs. Pepperpot's land from her neighbour's, but she knew the neighbour's dog quite well; he had had many a bone and scraps from her and he was always very friendly. 'We'll be all right here,' she thought.

But she was wrong. Without any warning, that dog suddenly came bearing down on them in great leaps and bounds! Mrs. Pepperpot shook like a jelly when she saw his wide-open jaws all red, with sharp, white teeth glistening in a terrifying way. She flattened herself on the cat's back and clung on for dear life, for Pussy shot like a Sputnik across the yard and straight under the neighbour's barn.

'Phew!' said the cat, 'that was a narrow squeak! Thanks very much for coming all this way with me; I'm afraid it wasn't a very comfortable journey.'

boys!' And they all started pelting snowballs as hard as they could.

Suddenly remembering how small she was, Mrs. Pepperpot did as the cat had told her and crouched down behind Pussy's ears until they were safely out of range.

The cat ran on till they got to a wire fence with a hole just big enough for her to wriggle through.

'That's all right,' said Mrs. Pepperpot, 'but perhaps you'll tell me now what we've come for?'

'It's a surprise,' said Pussy, 'but don't worry, you'll get your reward. All we have to do now is to find the hidden treasure, but that means crawling through the hay. So hang on!'

And off they went again, slowly this time, for it was difficult to make their way through the prickly stalks that seemed as big as bean-poles to Mrs. Pepperpot. The dust was terrible; it went in her eyes, her mouth, her hair, down her neck—everywhere.

'Can you see anything?' asked the cat.

'Only blackness,' answered Mrs. Pepperpot, 'and it seems to be getting blacker.'

'In that case we're probably going the right way,' said Pussy, crawling further into the hay. 'D'you see anything now?' she asked.

'Nothing at all,' said Mrs. Pepperpot, for by now her eyes were completely bunged up with hay-seed and dust.

'Try rubbing your eyes,' said the cat, 'for this is where your hidden treasure is.'

So Mrs. Pepperpot rubbed her eyes, blinked and rubbed again until at last she could open them properly. When she did, she was astonished; all round her shone the most wonderful jewels! Diamonds, sapphires, emeralds—they glittered in every hue!

'There you are! Didn't I tell you I had a hidden treasure for you?' said the cat, but she didn't give Mrs. Pepperpot time to have a closer look. 'We'll have to hurry back now, it's nearly time for your husband's dinner.'

So they crawled back through the hay and, just as they got out in the daylight, Mrs. Pepperpot grew to her ordinary size. She picked the cat up in her arms and walked across the yard with her. The dog was there, but what a different dog! He nuzzled Mrs. Pepperpot's skirt and wagged his tail in the friendliest way.

Through the gate they came to the place where the boys were playing. Everyone of them nodded to her and politely said 'Good morning'. Then they went on up the hill, and there were the magpies in the birch-tree. But not a sound came from them; they didn't even seem to notice them walking by.

When they got to the house Mrs. Pepperpot put the cat down and hurried indoors. It was almost one o'clock. She snatched the saucepan from the stove—a few potatoes had stuck to the bottom, so she threw those

out and emptied the rest into a blue serving-bowl. The saucepan she put outside the back door with cold water in it.

She had only just got everything ready when Mr. Pepperpot came in. He sniffed suspiciously. 'I can smell burnt potatoes,' he said.

'Nonsense,' said Mrs. Pepperpot, 'I dropped a bit of potato-skin on the stove, that's all. But I've aired the room since, so just you sit down and eat your dinner.'

'Aren't you having any?' asked her husband.

'Not just now,' answered Mrs. Pepperpot, 'I have to go and fetch something first. I won't be long.' And Mrs. Pepperpot went back down the hill, through the gate to her neighbour's yard, and into the barn. But this time she climbed *over* the hay till she found the spot where her hidden treasure lay.

And what d'you think it was?

Four coal-black kittens with shining eyes!

Mr. Pepperpot

Now you have heard a lot about *Mrs.* Pepperpot, but hardly anything about *Mr.* Pepperpot.

He usually comes in at the end of the stories, when Mrs. Pepperpot is back to her normal size and busy with his dinner. If the food isn't ready he always says 'Can't a man ever get his dinner at the proper time in this house?' And if it is ready, he just sits down to eat and says nothing at all. If it's cold out, he says 'Brrrrrrr!' and if it's very hot, he says 'Pheeew!' If Mrs. Pepperpot has done something he doesn't like, he says 'Hmmmmm!' in a disapproving tone of voice. But if he himself is thinking of doing something he doesn't want Mrs. Pepperpot to know about, he goes round the house whistling to himself and humming a little tune.

One evening when he came home, he went up to the attic. Now, Mrs. Pepperpot had hidden four black kittens up there, because Mr. Pepperpot didn't like kittens when they were small (some people don't, you know). So, when Mr. Pepperpot came down from the attic, he stood in the middle of the floor and said 'Hmmmm!' And a little while later he started whistling and humming his tune.

Mrs. Pepperpot said nothing, though she knew what it meant. She just took his old winter coat from its peg and started mending a tear in it.

'What are you mending that for?' asked Mr. Pepperpot.

'The weather's getting so bad, you'll need it,' said Mrs. Pepperpot.

'Who said I was going out?' asked Mr. Pepperpot.

'You can do as you like,' said his wife, 'I'm staying right where I am.'

'Well, maybe I *will* take a turn outside, all the same,' said Mr. Pepperpot.

'I thought you would,' she said.

Mr. Pepperpot went back to the attic, found a big sack and popped the four kittens inside. But when he got to the bottom of the stairs, he thought he would put on the old winter coat. So he put the sack down and went into the kitchen. There he found the coat hanging over a chair.

'I'm going out now!' he called, thinking his wife must be in the sitting-room. He got no answer, but he didn't bother to call again, as he was afraid the kittens might get out of the sack which wasn't properly tied. Quickly he slung it over his shoulder and went out.

It was a nasty night; the wind blew sleet in his face and the road was full of icy puddles.

'Ugh!' said Mr. Pepperpot, 'this weather's fit to drown in!'

'Isn't that just what you're going to do to us poor kittens?' said a tiny voice close by.

Mr. Pepperpot was startled. 'Who said that, I wonder?' he said. He put the sack down to look inside, but as soon as he opened it out jumped one of the kittens and ran off in the darkness.

'Oh dear, what shall I do?' he said, tying up the sack again as quickly as he could. 'I can't leave a kitten running about on a night like this.'

'He won't get any wetter than the rest of us by the time you've finished with us,' said the little voice again.

Mr. Pepperpot untied the sack once more to find out who was speaking. Out jumped the second kitten and disappeared in the sleet and snow. While he hurriedly tied a knot to stop the rest from getting out, he said to himself:

'What if the fox got those two little mites? That would be terrible!'

'No worse than being in *your* hands,' said the tiny voice.

This time, Mr. Pepperpot was very careful to hold his hand over the opening as he untied it. But his foot slipped on the ice and jogged the sack out of his hand, and another kitten got away.

'Three gone! That's bad!' he said.

'Not as bad as it'll be for me!' came the voice from the sack.

'I know who it is now,' said Mr. Pepperpot; 'it's my

old woman who's shrunk again. You're in that sack, aren't you? But I'll catch you! You just wait!' And with that he opened the sack again.

Out jumped the fourth kitten and ran off, lickety-split!

'You can run, I don't care!' said the old man. 'I'm going to catch that wife of mine—it's all her fault!' He got down on his knees and rummaged round in every corner of the sack. But he found nothing—it was quite empty.

Now he really was worried; he was so worried he started sobbing and crying, and in between he called 'Puss, Puss!' and searched all over the place.

A little girl came along the road. 'What have you lost?' she asked.

'Some kittens,' sniffed Mr. Pepperpot.

'I'll help you find them,' said the little girl.

Soon they were joined by a little boy, and he had a torch which made it easier to search. First the little girl found one kitten behind a tree-stump, then the boy found two kittens stuck in a snow-drift, and Mr. Pepperpot himself found the fourth one and put them all back in the sack, tying it very securely this time.

'Thank you for your help,' he said to the children and asked them to take the kittens back to his house and put them in the kitchen.

When they had gone, he started looking for his little old woman. He searched for an hour—for two hours; he called, he begged, he sobbed, he was quite beside himself. But in the end he had to give up. 'I'll go home now,' he said to himself, 'and try again tomorrow.'

But when he got home, there was Mrs. Pepperpot, as large as life, bustling round the kitchen, frying a huge pile of pancakes! And by the kitchen stove was a wicker basket with the mother cat and all four kittens in it.

'When did you come home?' asked the astonished Mr. Pepperpot.

'When did I come home? Why, I've been here all the time, of course,' she said.

'But who was it talking to me from the sack, then?'

'I've no idea,' said Mrs. Pepperpot, 'unless it was your conscience.' And she came over and gave him a great big hug and kiss.

Then Mr. Pepperpot sat down to eat the biggest pile of pancakes he had ever had and all with bilberry jam, and when he was full the kittens finished off the last four.

And after that Mr. and Mrs. Pepperpot lived happily together, and Mrs. Pepperpot gave up shrinking for a very long time indeed.

Mrs Pepperpot to the Rescue

WHEN IT IS breaking-up day at the village school, and the summer holidays are about to begin, all the children bring flowers to decorate the school. They pick them in their own gardens or they get them from their uncles and aunts, and then they carry their big bunches along the road, while they sing and shout because it is the end of term. Their mothers and fathers wave to them from the windows and wish them a happy breaking-up day.

But in one window stands a little old woman who just watches the children go by. That is Mrs Pepperpot.

She has no one now to wish a happy breaking-up day, for all her own children are long since grown up and gone away, and none of the young ones think of asking her for flowers.

At least, that's not quite true; I do know of one little girl who picked flowers in Mrs Pepperpot's garden. But that was several years ago, not long after the little old woman first started shrinking to the size of a pepperpot at the most inconvenient moments.

That particular summer Mrs Pepperpot's garden was fairly bursting with flowers: there were white lilac with boughs almost laden to the ground, blue and red anemones on strong, straight stalks, poppies with graceful nodding yellow heads and many other lovely flowers. But no one had asked Mrs Pepperpot for any of them, so she just stood in her window and watched as the children went by, singing and shouting, on their way to the breaking-up day at school.

The very last to cross the yard in front of her house was a little girl, and she was walking, oh, so slowly, and

carried nothing in her hands. Mrs Pepperpot's cat was lying on the doorstep and greeted her with a 'Miaow!' But the little girl only made a face and said, 'Stupid animal!' And when Mrs Pepperpot's dog, which was chained to the wall, started barking and wagging his tail the little girl snapped, 'Hold your tongue!'

Then Mrs Pepperpot opened the window to throw a bone out to the dog and the little girl whirled round and shouted angrily, 'Don't you throw that dirty bone on my dress!'

That was enough. Mrs Pepperpot put her hands on her hips and told the little girl that no one had any right to cross the yard in front of her house and throw insulting words at her or her cat and dog, which were doing no harm to anybody.

The little girl began to cry. 'I want to go home,' she sobbed. 'I've an awful pain in my tummy and I don't want to go to the breaking-up party! Why should I go when I have a pain in my tummy?'

'Where's your mother, child?' asked Mrs Pepperpot.

'None of your business!' snapped the girl.

'Well, where's your father, then?' asked Mrs Pepperpot.

'Never you mind!' said the girl, still more rudely. 'But if you want to know why I don't want to go to school today it's because I haven't any flowers. We haven't a garden, anyway, as we've only been here since Christmas. But Dad's going to build us a house now that he's working at the ironworks, and then we'll have a garden. My mum makes paper flowers and does the paper round, see? Anything more you'd like to know? Oh well, I might as well go to school, I suppose. Teacher can say what she likes—I don't care! If *she'd* been going from school to school for three years she wouldn't know much either! So blow her and her flowers!' And the little girl stared defiantly at Mrs Pepperpot.

Mrs Pepperpot stared back at the little girl and then

she said: 'That's the spirit! But I think I can help you with the flowers. Just you go out in the garden and pick some lilac and anemones and poppies and anything else you like. I'll go and find some paper for you to wrap them in.'

So the girl went into the garden and started picking flowers while Mrs Pepperpot went indoors for some paper. But just as she was coming back to the door she shrank!

Roly Poly! And there she was, tucked up in the paper like jam in a pudding, when the little girl came running back with her arms full of flowers.

'Here we are!' shouted the little girl.

'And here *we* are!' said Mrs Pepperpot as she disentangled herself from the paper. 'Don't be scared; this is something that happens to me from time to time, and I never know when I'm going to shrink. But now I've got an idea; I want you to pop me in your satchel and take me along with you to school. We're going to have a game with them all! What's your name, by the way?'

'It's Rita,' said the little girl who was staring at Mrs Pepperpot with open mouth.

'Well, Rita, don't just stand there. Hurry up and put the paper round those flowers. There's no time to lose!'

When they got to the school the breaking-up party was well under way, and the teacher didn't look particularly pleased even when Rita handed her the lovely bunch of flowers. She just nodded and said, 'Thanks.'

'Take no notice,' said Mrs Pepperpot from Rita's satchel.

'Go to your desk,' said the teacher. Rita sat down with her satchel on her knee.

'We'll start with a little arithmetic,' said the teacher. 'What are seven times seven?'

'Forty-nine!' whispered Mrs Pepperpot from the satchel.

'Forty-nine!' said Rita.

This made the whole class turn round and stare at Rita, for up to now she had hardly been able to count to thirty! But Rita stared back at them and smiled. Then she stole a quick look at her satchel.

'What's that on your lap?' asked the teacher. 'Nobody is allowed to use a crib. Give me your satchel at once!'

So Rita had to carry it up to the teacher's desk where it was hung on a peg.

The teacher went on to the next question: 'If we take fifteen from eighteen what do we get?'

All the children started counting on their fingers, but Rita saw that Mrs Pepperpot was sticking both her arms and one leg out of the satchel.

'Three!' said Rita before the others had had time to answer.

This time nobody suspected her of cheating and Rita beamed all over while Mrs Pepperpot waved to her from between the pages of her exercise book.

'Very strange, I must say,' said the teacher. 'Now we'll have a little history and geography. Which country is it that has a long wall running round it and has the oldest culture in the world?'

Rita was watching the satchel the whole time, and now she saw Mrs Pepperpot's head pop up again. The little old woman had smeared her face with yellow chalk and now she put her fingers in the corners of her eyes and pulled them into narrow slits.

'China!' shouted Rita.

The teacher was quite amazed at this answer, but she had to admit that Rita was right. Then she made an announcement.

'Children,' she said, 'I have decided to award a treat to the one of you who gave the most right answers. Rita gave me all the right answers, so she is the winner, and she will be allowed to serve coffee to the teachers in the staff-room afterwards.'

Rita felt very pleased and proud; she was so used to getting meals ready when she was alone at home that she was sure she could manage this all right. So, when the other children went home, she took her satchel from the teacher's desk and went out into the kitchen. But, oh dear, it wasn't a bit like home! The coffee-pot was far too big and the huge cake with icing on it was very different from the plate of bread-and-dripping she usually got ready for her parents at home. Luckily the cups and saucers and plates and spoons had all been laid out on the table beforehand. All the same, it seemed too much to Rita, and she just sat down and cried. In a moment she heard the sound of scratching from the satchel, and out stepped Mrs Pepperpot.

'If you're the girl I take you for,' said the little old woman, putting her hands on her hips, 'you won't give up half-way like this! Come on, just you lift me up on the table, we'll soon have this job done! As far as I could see from my hiding place, there are nine visiting teachers and your own Miss Snooty. That makes two cups of water and two dessertspoons of coffee per person—which makes twenty cups of water and twenty dessertspoons of coffee in all—right?'

'I think so. Oh, you're wonderful!' said Rita, drying her tears. 'I'll measure out the water and coffee at once, but I don't know how I'm going to cut up that cake!'

'That'll be all right,' said Mrs. Pepperpot. 'As far as I can see the cake is about ninety paces—my paces—round. So if we divide it by ten that'll make each piece nine paces. But that will be too big for each slice, so we'll divide nine by three and make each piece three paces thick. Right?'

'I expect so,' said Rita, who was getting a bit lost.

'But first we must mark a circle in the middle of the cake,' went on Mrs Pepperpot. 'Lift me up on your hand, please.'

Rita lifted her carefully on to her hand.

'Now take me by the legs and turn me upside down. Then, while you swing me round, I can mark a circle with one finger in the icing. Right; let's go!'

So Rita swung Mrs Pepperpot round upside down and the result was a perfect little circle drawn right in the middle of the cake.

'Crumbs are better than no bread!' said Mrs Pepperpot as she stood there, swaying giddily and licking her finger. 'Now I'll walk right round the cake, and at every third step I want you to make a little notch in the icing with the knife. Here we go!

'One, two, three, notch!
One, two, three, notch!
One, two, three, notch!'

And in this way Mrs Pepperpot marched all round the cake, and Rita notched it so that it made exactly thirty slices when it was cut.

When they had finished someone called from the staff-room: 'Where's that clever girl with the coffee? Hurry up and bring it in, dear, then you can fetch the cake afterwards.'

Rita snatched up the big coffee-pot, which was boiling now, and hurried in with it, and Mrs Pepperpot stood listening to the way the teachers praised Rita as she poured the coffee into the cups with a steady hand.

After a while she came out for the cake. Mrs Pepperpot clapped her hands: 'Well done, Rita! There's nothing to worry about now.'

But she shouldn't have said that, for while she was listening to the teachers telling Rita again how clever she was, she suddenly heard that Miss Snooty raising her voice:

'I'm afraid you've forgotten two things, dear,' she said.

'Oh dear!' thought Mrs Pepperpot, 'the cream-jug and the sugar-bowl! I shall have to look and see if they are both filled.'

The cream-jug was full, but when Mrs Pepperpot leaned over the edge of the sugar-bowl she toppled in! And at the same moment Rita rushed in, put the lid on the sugar-bowl and put it and the cream-jug on a little tray. Then she turned round and went back to the staff-room.

First Mrs Pepperpot wondered if she should tell Rita where she was, but she was afraid the child might drop the tray altogether, so instead she buried herself well down in the sugar-bowl and hoped for the best.

Rita started carrying the tray round. But her teacher hadn't finished with her yet. 'I hope you remembered the sugar-tongs,' she said.

Rita didn't know what to say, but Mrs Pepperpot heard the remark, and when the visiting head teacher took the lid off, Mrs Pepperpot popped up like a jack-in-the-box holding a lump of sugar in her outstretched hand. She stared straight in front of her and never moved

an eyelid, so the head teacher didn't notice anything odd. He simply took the sugar lump and waved Rita on with the tray. But his neighbour at the table looked hard at Mrs Pepperpot and said: 'What very curious sugar-tongs—I suppose they're made of plastic. Whatever will they think of next?' Then he asked Rita if she had brought them with her from home, and she said yes, which was strictly true, of course.

After that everyone wanted to have a look at the curious sugar-tongs, till in the end Rita's teacher called her over.

'Let me have a look at those tongs,' she said. She reached out her hand to pick them up, but this was too much for Mrs Pepperpot. In a moment she had the whole tray over and everything fell on the floor. The

cream-jug was smashed and the contents of the sugar-bowl rolled under the cupboard, which was just as well for Mrs Pepperpot!

But the teacher thought it was she who had upset the tray, and suddenly she was sorry she had been so hard on the little girl. She put her arms round Rita and gave her a hug. 'It was all my fault,' she said. 'You've been a very good little parlourmaid.'

Later, when all the guests had gone, and Rita was clearing the table, the teacher pointed to the dark corner by the cupboard and said, 'Who is that standing there?'

And out stepped Mrs Pepperpot as large as life and quite unruffled. 'I've been sent to lend a hand with the washing-up,' she said. 'Give me that tray, Rita. You and I will go out into the kitchen.'

When at last the two of them were walking home, Rita said, 'Why did you help me all day when I was so horrid to you this morning?'

'Well,' said Mrs Pepperpot, 'perhaps it was because you *were* so horrid. Next time maybe I'll help that Miss Snooty of yours. She looks pretty horrid too, but she might be nice underneath.'

Mrs Pepperpot on the Warpath

IT WAS the day after Mrs Pepperpot had helped Rita at the school party, and the little old woman was in a terrible rage. You see, if there's anything Mrs Pepperpot hates, it's people being unkind to children. All night she had been thinking about it, and now she had made up her mind to go and tell Rita's teacher just what she thought of her. So she put on her best hat and her best frock, straightened her back and marched off to the school.

'I hope I don't shrink this time,' she thought, 'but it's not likely to happen two days running. Anyway, today I must have my say or I shall burst. Somebody's going to say she's sorry or my name's not Pepperpot!'

She had reached the school gate and swung it open. Then she walked up to the teacher's front door and knocked twice smartly. Then she waited.

No one said, 'Come in!'

Mrs Pepperpot knocked again, but there was still no answer. So she decided to try the latch. 'If the door isn't locked I shall go straight in,' she said to herself. She pressed the latch and the door opened. But no sooner had she put a foot over the threshold than she shrank and fell head over heels into a travelling-rug which was rolled up on the floor just inside the door! Next to it stood a suitcase and a hatbox.

'Oh, calamity!' cried Mrs Pepperpot, 'let's hope she's not in after all now!' But she was unlucky, for now she could hear footsteps in the corridor and the teacher came towards the front door dressed in her going-out clothes.

'What an old dolt I am!' thought Mrs Pepperpot. 'Fancy me not remembering the summer holidays have started today and she'll be going away, of course. Oh well, she's not gone yet. If I can manage to stay near her

for a little while longer I may still get my chance to give her a piece of my mind.' So she hid in the rug.

The teacher picked up the suitcase in one hand, then she threw the travelling-rug over her shoulder and picked up the hatbox in the other hand and walked out of the house, closing the door behind her. And Mrs Pepperpot? She was clinging for dear life to the fringe of the rug and she was still as angry as ever.

'Very nice, I must say!' she muttered. 'Going away on a holiday like this without a thought for Rita and all the harm you did her. But you wait, my fine lady, very soon it'll be my turn to teach you a thing or two!'

The teacher walked briskly on, with Mrs Pepperpot dangling behind her, till they got to the station. Then she walked over to the fruit-stall and put the rug down on the counter, and Mrs Pepperpot was able to slip out of it and hide behind a bunch of flowers.

The teacher asked for two pounds of apples.

'That's right!' fumed Mrs Pepperpot to herself. 'Buy two pounds of apples to gorge yourself with on the train!'

'And eight oranges, please,' continued the teacher.

'Worse and worse!' muttered Mrs Pepperpot.

'And three pounds of bananas, please,' said the teacher.

Mrs Pepperpot could hardly contain herself: 'If I was my proper size now, I'd give you apples and oranges and bananas, and no mistake!'

Then the teacher said to the lady in the fruit-stall:

'Do you think you could do me a favour? I want all this fruit to go to one of my pupils, but I have to catch the train, so I've no time to take it to her myself. Could you deliver it to Rita Johansen in the little house by the church and tell her it's from me?'

On hearing this, Mrs Pepperpot's ears nearly fell off with astonishment. It was just as if someone had taken a sweet out of her mouth and left her nothing to suck; what was she going to say now?

'I'll do that for you with pleasure, miss,' said the fruit-lady. 'That'll be twelve shillings exactly.'

'Oh dear!' exclaimed the teacher, rummaging in her purse, 'I see I shan't have enough money left after buying my ticket. Would you mind if I owed you the twelve shillings till I come back from my holidays?'

'The very idea! Asking me to deliver goods you can't

even pay for! I shall have to have the fruit back, please,' the fruit-lady said, and held out her hand.

The teacher said she was sorry, put the bag of fruit back on the counter and went off to board her train, but Mrs Pepperpot had taken the chance to jump into the bag.

Silently she wished the teacher a good holiday: 'You're not so bad after all, and you needn't worry; I'll see that Rita gets her bag of fruit somehow. But *somebody's* going to get the edge of my tongue before the day's out!'

Of course the fruit-lady could no more hear what Mrs Pepperpot was saying than the teacher could. She was busy getting ready to shut up shop and go home. But when she had put her hat on and opened the door she suddenly turned round and picked up the bag of fruit on the counter.

Mrs Pepperpot had just been wondering if she was going to be locked in the fruit-stall all night, and now here she was, being taken on another journey!

'I suppose you're going to eat all this yourself, you selfish old thing, you!' thought Mrs Pepperpot, getting worked up again. 'The teacher may be snooty, but at least she has a kind heart underneath. You're just plain mean! But just you wait till I grow again!'

The fruit-lady walked on and on, until at last Mrs

Pepperpot could hear her opening a door and going into a room. There she set the bag down with a thump on the table, and Mrs Pepperpot was able to climb over an orange and peep out of the top.

She saw a man banging on the table, and he was as cross as a sore bear. 'What sort of time is this to come home?' he roared. 'I've been waiting and waiting for my supper. Hurry up now! What's in that bag, anyway?'

'Oh, it's only some fruit for a little girl,' said his wife. 'The school-teacher wanted to send it to Rita Johansen, but she found she hadn't enough money, so I took it back. Then when she'd gone I felt sorry, so I thought I'd take it along to the child myself.'

This time Mrs Pepperpot was really amazed: 'Well, I never!' she gasped, 'here's another one who turns out to be nice. Still, I'm sure her husband won't; he looks as if he could do with a good ticking off!'

The fruit-lady's husband certainly was a cross-patch and no mistake. He banged his fist on the table and shouted that no wife of his was going to waste money and time running errands for silly school-teachers and brats.

'Give me that bag!' he roared. 'I'll take it right back to the shop this minute!' And he snatched up the bag from the table. Poor Mrs Pepperpot was given an awful shaking and landed up jammed between two bananas.

Taking long strides, the man walked off down the road.

'Bye-bye, fruit-lady!' whispered Mrs Pepperpot. 'You have a nasty husband, but I'll deal with him shortly, don't you worry!'

Squeezed and bruised, the little old woman lay there in the bag while the man strode on. But after a while he walked more slowly and at last he stopped at a house and knocked on the door.

'Surely this isn't the station?' wondered Mrs Pepperpot.

129

She heard the door open and the man spoke: 'Are you Rita Johansen?'

Then she heard a little girl's voice, 'Yes, that's me.'

'Your teacher sent you this,' said the man and handed over the bag; 'it's fruit.'

'Oh, thank you!' said Rita. 'I'll just go and get a bowl to put it in.' And she set the bag on a chair.

'That's all right,' said the man, and he turned on his heel and walked away.

When Rita came back with the bowl she thought she heard the door close, but she didn't take much notice in her eagerness to see what the teacher had sent her.

But it was actually Mrs Pepperpot who had slipped out, for she was now her usual size and she wanted time to think; it had all been so surprising and not at all what she expected. As she walked she began to hurry. For now she knew who was going to get a piece of her mind, and rightly so! Someone who made her more angry than anyone else just now!

When she got home she marched straight to the mirror. Putting her hands on her hips she glared at the little old woman she saw there. 'Well!' she said, 'and who do you think you are, running round the country-side, poking your nose in where you're not wanted? Is it any of your business, may I ask, who the school-teacher buys fruit for? What d'you mean by hiding in people's travelling-rugs and spying on them? You ought to be ashamed of yourself, an old woman like you, behaving like a senseless child. As for the fruit-lady, why shouldn't she be cross? How was she to know if she could trust the teacher? And her husband; I suppose he can bang his fist on his own table if he likes without you interfering? Are you listening? Wouldn't you be pretty mad if you'd come home hungry and the wife wasn't there to cook your meal, eh? I'm disgusted with you! *They* were sorry for what they did and made amends, all three of them, but *you*, you just stand there glaring at me as if nothing had happened. Wouldn't it be an idea to say you were sorry?'

Mrs Pepperpot turned her back on the mirror and took a deep breath. 'That's better!' she said. 'I've got it all off my chest at last. Now I can give my tongue a rest and get on with the housework.'

But first she took one more look in the mirror, smiled shyly and bobbed a little curtsy.

'I'm sorry!' she said.

And the little old woman in the mirror smiled back at her and bobbed a little curtsy too.

The Nature Lesson

EVERY MORNING, when Mrs Pepperpot sits at her window with her after-breakfast cup of coffee, she watches a little boy who always walks across her yard on his way to school. The boy's name is Olly and he and Mrs Pepperpot are very good friends, though not in the way grown-ups usually are friends with children. Quite often Olly rushes past Mrs Pepperpot's window without even saying 'Good morning', because he is in such a hurry. But then Mrs Pepperpot has never even asked him his name or how old he is or what he wants for Christmas. She just watches him every morning and says to herself, 'There goes the little boy on his way to school.' As for Olly, he just glances up at her window and thinks, 'There's the old woman, drinking her coffee.'

Now with animals it is different: if Olly sees the cat sitting on Mrs Pepperpot's door-step he can't resist stopping to stroke her. He'll even sit down on the door-step and talk to her.

'Hullo, pussy,' he'll say. 'There's a lovely pussy!' And then, of course, he has to go and see the dog outside his kennel as well, in case he should get jealous.

'Hullo, boy! Good dog, good dog! You didn't think I'd forgotten you, did you? Oh, I wouldn't do that! There's a good dog!' And by the time he's made a fuss of them both he's late for school.

This is Olly's trouble: he's *very* fond of animals. He loves to play hide-and-seek with the squirrel he sees on his way to school, or to have a whistling-match with a blackbird. And as for *rainy* days, well, he spends so much time trying not to step on the worms wriggling by the puddles in the road that he's *always* late for school.

This won't do, of course, and when he's late his teacher gets cross, and she'll say, 'It's all very well being fond of animals; it's quite right that you should be, but it's no excuse for being late for school.'

But that wasn't what I was going to tell you. What I was going to tell you was how Mrs Pepperpot had a nature lesson one day. So here we go!

It was a lovely spring day, and Mrs Pepperpot was sitting by the window as usual, enjoying her cup of coffee and watching Olly come across the yard. He was walking rather briskly this time—watching some bird or animal had probably made him late again—so he had

only time to say 'Hullo, puss!' to the cat on the door-step and 'Hi, boy!' to the dog by the kennel.

But suddenly he stopped dead, turned round on his heel and started running back across the yard. Mrs Pepperpot had just come to the door to give the dog his breakfast and Olly rushed past her as fast as he could go.

Mrs Pepperpot called to him: 'Whatever's the matter with you, boy? The police after you?'

'Forgot my nature textbook!' answered Olly over his shoulder, and started off again.

'Wait a minute!' called Mrs Pepperpot. Olly stopped. 'You can't go all the way home again now; you'll be much too late for school. No, you go on and *I'll* go back for your book and bring it to you at school.'

Olly shuffled his feet a bit and looked unhappy; he didn't much like the idea of an old woman turning up in school with his nature textbook.

'Don't stand there shuffling, boy!' said Mrs Pepperpot. 'Where did you leave the book?'

'On the window-sill,' he answered; 'the window is open.'

'All right. Where do you want me to put the book when I get to the school? Come on, hurry up; we haven't got all day!' said Mrs Pepperpot, trying to look severe.

'There's a hole in the wall, just by the big birch tree; there's an old bird-nest there you can put it in.'

'In the old nest in a hole in the wall by the birch tree; right!' said Mrs Pepperpot. 'Now, off you go and see if you can be on time for a change! I'll see to the rest.'

'Righto!' said Olly and was off before you could say Jack Robinson.

Mrs Pepperpot took off her apron, smoothed her hair and stepped out into the yard. And then, of course, the inevitable thing happened; she shrank!

'This is bad,' thought Mrs Pepperpot, as she peeped over the wet grass by the door-step, 'but I've known worse.' She called to the cat: 'Come here, puss! You'll have to be my horse once again and help me fetch Olly's nature book from his house.'

'Miaow! All right,' said the cat, as she allowed Mrs Pepperpot to climb on her back. 'What sort of a thing is a nature book?'

'It's a book the children use in school to learn about animals,' answered Mrs Pepperpot, 'and one thing it says about cats is that you are "carnivores".'

'What does that mean?' asked the cat.

'That you eat meat, but never mind that now; all you have to do is to take me straight down the road till we get to the stream. Then we take a short cut across. . . .'

But, as they came near the stream, the cat said, 'Doesn't the book say anything about cats not liking to get their feet wet?' And then she stopped so abruptly that poor Mrs Pepperpot toppled right over her head and fell plump into the water!

'Good job I can swim,' spluttered Mrs Pepperpot as she came to the surface, 'humans aren't meant to live under water on account of the way they breathe with their lungs. Phew! It's hard work all the same; I'll take a rest on this stone and see if something turns up.'

While she was getting her breath a tiny animal stuck its nose out of the water, and started snarling at her. Now Mrs Pepperpot knew what that was, but you probably wouldn't, because it only lives in the faraway places, and it is called a lemming. Its fur is dappled brown and fawn, so that it looks a bit like a guinea-pig in summer, but in winter it turns white as the snow around it.

As I say, Mrs Pepperpot knew all about lemmings, so she snarled back at the little creature, making as horrible a noise as she could. 'I'm not afraid of you!' she said, 'though the book says you're the worst-tempered of all the little rodents and don't give way to a fierce dog or even a grown man. But now you can just stop showing off and help me out of this stream like a good lemming.'

'Well, blow me down!' said the lemming. 'I never saw a woman as small as you and with such a loud voice. Get on my back and I'll take you across. Where are you going, by the way?'

'To fetch a nature book from the house over there for a little boy at school,' said Mrs Pepperpot. 'And in that book there is quite a bit about you.'

'Oh? And what does it say?' asked the lemming, crawling out on to the grass with Mrs Pepperpot.

'It says that once every so many years lemmings come down from the mountains in great swarms and eat up all the green stuff they can find till they get to the sea.' Then she stopped, because she remembered that when the lemmings reach the sea in their search for food, thousands of them get drowned.

'We do get rather hungry,' said the lemming; 'as a matter of fact, I'm on my way now to join my mates in a little food-hunt. . . .'

'Couldn't you just take me down to the house?' pleaded Mrs Pepperpot; she didn't like the idea that he might drown in the sea. But the lemming's empty tummy was telling him to go, so he told Mrs Pepperpot she would have to manage by herself, and he ran off muttering to himself about juicy green leaves.

Before Mrs Pepperpot had had time to wonder what

would happen to him, another head appeared above a little wall. This time it was a stoat.

'Hullo, Mr Nosey Parker,' she greeted him, 'what are you looking for?'

'I thought you were a mouse, but I see you're a little old woman, and I don't eat women,' said the stoat. 'Have you by any chance got a silver spoon?' he added.

'I have something you like even better than silver spoons,' answered Mrs Pepperpot, 'a whole packet of tin-tacks, and you can have them if you'll take me to that house over there. I have to fetch a book from the window-sill for a little boy in the school.'

'All right,' said the stoat, 'hop up!'

So Mrs Pepperpot got on his back. But it was a most

uncomfortable journey, because stoats, like weasels, move by rippling their long bodies, and though they have short legs, they can run very fast. Mrs Pepperpot had a job keeping on and was glad when they reached the wall under the window.

The stoat scrambled up to the window-sill, and presently he came back with the book—under his chin.

'Why do you carry the book that way?' asked Mrs Pepperpot.

'How else?' answered the stout. 'I always carry eggs under my chin.'

'Eggs?' Mrs Pepperpot pretended to be surprised. 'I didn't know stoats laid eggs.'

'Ha, ha, very funny!' said the stoat. 'I suppose you don't eat eggs?'

'Oh yes,' said Mrs Pepperpot, 'but I don't steal them out of wild birds' nests.'

'That's my business,' said the stoat. 'Now you'd better think how you're going to get this book to school; I can't carry both you and the book.'

'That's true!' said Mrs Pepperpot. 'I'll have to think of something.'

But it wasn't necessary, for the next moment Mrs Pepperpot was back to her proper size. As she bent down to pick up the book she whispered to the little stoat, 'The tin-tacks will be waiting for you in that nest you robbed in the stone wall by the school.' And she thought she heard him chuckle as he rippled away in the grass.

When she reached the school the bell was ringing for break, and she just had time to pop the book into the empty nest before Olly came running out with the other children. Mrs Pepperpot gave the tiniest nod in the direction of the wall and then she walked briskly away.

But the next morning Olly brought a lovely bone for her dog and from his milk bottle he poured a good saucer-full of milk for her pussy.

Mrs Pepperpot opened the window. 'Would you do something for me this morning?' she asked.

'As long as it won't make me late for school,' answered Olly.

'Good,' said Mrs Pepperpot. Then she fetched a packet of tin-tacks from the toolshed and gave them to Olly. 'Put those in the empty nest in the wall, will you? They're for a friend of mine.'

Mrs Pepperpot is taken for a Witch

MRS PEPPERPOT lives in a valley in Norway, and in summertime in that part of the world the nights hardly get dark at all. On Midsummer's Eve, in fact, the sun never quite goes down, so everybody, young and old, stays up all night to dance and sing and let off fireworks round a big bonfire. And because there's magic abroad on Midsummer's Eve they sometimes see witches riding on broomsticks through the sky—or they think they do, anyway.

Now the only two people in that valley who never used to go to the bonfire party were Mr and Mrs Pepperpot. Not that Mrs Pepperpot didn't want to go, but Midsummer's Eve happened to be Mr Pepperpot's birthday as well, and on that day it was he who decided what they did. He never liked mixing with a crowd on account of that shrinking habit of Mrs Pepperpot; he was always afraid that she would suddenly turn the size of a pepperpot and disappear, leaving him standing there looking a proper fool.

But this year Mrs Pepperpot *did* go to the party, and this is how it happened.

It started the night before Midsummer's Eve. Mrs Pepperpot had been to the store and was walking slowly home with her basket on her arm. She was wondering how she could persuade her husband to go to the bonfire when suddenly she had an idea.

'I could ask him if there was something he really wanted for his birthday, and then I could say I would give it to him if he promised to take me to the bonfire party.'

As soon as she got inside the door she jumped on her husband's knee and gave him a smacking kiss on the tip of his nose.

'Dear, good hubby,' she said, 'have you got a very special wish for your birthday tomorrow?'

Her husband was quite surprised. 'Have you had sun-stroke or something? How could you buy anything? Why, money runs through your fingers like water.'

'Sometimes it does, and sometimes it doesn't,' said Mrs Pepperpot, looking sly; 'there are such things as hens, and hens lay eggs and eggs can be sold. Just now I have quite a tidy sum put by, so just you tell me what you would like and the present will be laid out here on the table as sure as my name's Pepperpot.'

'Well,' he said, 'if you think you have enough money to buy that handsome pipe with the silver band that's lying in the store window, I'll promise you something in return.'

'Done!' cried Mrs Pepperpot at once, 'and the thing I want you to promise me is to take me to the bonfire party on Windy Ridge tomorrow night!'

So Mr Pepperpot had to agree and the next day Mrs Pepperpot filled her pockets with all the sixpennies, pennies and threepenny bits she had earned from the eggs and set off to the store.

'I want to buy the pipe with the silver band,' said Mrs Pepperpot, when it came to her turn to be served.

But the grocer shook his head. 'Sorry, Mrs Pepperpot,'

he said, 'but I'm afraid I sold that pipe to Peter Poulsen yesterday.'

'Oh dear,' said Mrs Pepperpot, 'I'll have to go and see if he'll let me buy it off him,' and she hurried out of the door, letting the door-bell jingle loudly as she went.

She took the shortest way to Peter Poulsen's house, but when she got there only his wife was at home.

'I was wondering if your husband would sell me that pipe he bought in the store yesterday?' said Mrs Pepperpot. 'I'd pay him well for it,' she added, and patted her pocketful of coins.

'That pipe is no longer in the house,' said Mrs Poulsen, who had a sour look on her face. 'I wasn't going to have tobacco smoke in my curtains, no *thank* you! I gave it to some boys who were having a sale; they said they were collecting money for fireworks for tonight's bonfire, or some such nonsense.'

Mrs Pepperpot's heart sank; did Mrs Poulsen know where the sale was being held?

'Up on Windy Ridge, near the bonfire, the boys said,' answered Mrs Poulsen, and Mrs Pepperpot lost no time in making her way up to Windy Ridge.

But it was a tidy walk uphill and when she got to the top she found the boys had sold everything. They were busy tidying up the bits of paper and string and cardboard boxes and carrying them over to the bonfire.

Mrs Pepperpot was so out of breath her tongue was hanging out, but she managed to stammer, 'Who got the pipe?'

'What pipe?' asked one of the boys.

'The one with the silver band that Mrs Poulsen gave you.'

'Oh that,' said the boy; 'my brother bought it. But then he tried to smoke it and it made him sick. So he got fed up with it and tied it to a long pole and stuck it at the top of the bonfire. There it is—look!'

Mrs Pepperpot looked, and there it was, right enough, tied to a pole at the very top of the huge bonfire!

'Couldn't you take it down again?' she asked the boy.

'Are you crazy?' said the boy. 'Expect us to upset the bonfire when we've got everything piled up just nicely? Not likely! Besides, we're going to have some fun with that pipe; you wait and see! But I can't stand talking now, I must go and get a can of petrol to start it off.' And he ran off with the other boys.

'Oh dear, oh dear, oh dear!' wailed Mrs Pepperpot

to herself. 'I see there's nothing for it but to climb that bonfire and get it down myself.' But she looked with dismay at the mountain of old mattresses, broken chairs, table-legs, barrows, drawers, old clothes and hats, car-tyres and empty cartons.

'First I shall have to find a stick to poke the pipe off the pole when I do get up aloft,' she thought.

Just at that moment she turned small, but for once Mrs Pepperpot was really pleased. 'Hooray!' she shouted in her shrill little voice. 'It won't take long for a little thing like me to get that pipe down now, and I don't even need to upset the bonfire!'

Quick as a mouse, she darted into the big pile and started climbing up from the inside. But it was not as easy as she had thought; climbing over a mattress she got her heel stuck in a spring and it took her quite a while to free herself. Then she had difficulty in climbing a slippery chair-leg; she kept sliding back. But at last she managed it, only to find herself entangled in the lining of a coat. She groped about in this for some time before she found her way out of the sleeve.

By now people had started gathering round the bonfire.

'All right, let them have a good look,' she thought. 'Luckily I'm too small for them to see me up here. And nothing's going to stop me from getting to the top now!'

Just then she lost her grip and fell into a deep drawer. There she lay, puffing and blowing, till she managed to catch hold of a bonnet string which was hanging over the edge of the drawer.

'Not much further to go, thank goodness!' she told herself, but when she looked down she almost fainted; it was fearfully far to the ground, and now there were crowds of people standing round, waiting for the bonfire to be lit.

'No time to lose!' thought Mrs Pepperpot, and heaved herself on to the last obstacle. This was easy, because it was an old concertina, so she could walk up it like a staircase.

Now she was at the foot of the pole and at the top was the pipe, securely tied!

'However am I going to get up there?' she wondered, but then she noticed the rim of an empty tar-barrel right next to her. So she smeared a little tar on her hands to give them a better grip, and then she started to climb the pole. But the pole and the whole bonfire seemed to be heeling a little over to one side, and when she looked down she nearly fell off with fright: *the boys had lit the bonfire!*

Little flames were licking up round the mattresses and the broken furniture.

Then people started cheering and the children chanted: 'Wait till it gets to the pipe at the top! Wait till it gets to the pipe at the top!'

'Catch me waiting!' muttered Mrs Pepperpot. 'I've got to get there *first*!' and she climbed on up till her hands gripped the stem of the pipe. Down below she could hear the children shouting:

'Watch the flames when they reach the pole! There's a rocket tied to the pipe!'

'Oh, good gracious!' cried Mrs Pepperpot, clinging on for dear life. BANG! Up into the cold night sky shot the rocket, the pole, the pipe *and* Mrs Pepperpot!

Round the bonfire everyone suddenly stopped shouting. A thin woman in a shawl whispered to her neighbour:

'I thought I saw someone sitting on that stick!'

Her neighbour, who was even thinner and wore two shawls, whispered back, 'It could have been a witch!' and they both shuddered. But from behind them came a man's voice:

'Oh, it couldn't be her, could it?' It was Mr Pepperpot who had just left off working and had taken a ride up to the mountain to have a look at the bonfire. Now he swung himself on his bicycle again and raced home as fast as he could go, muttering all the way, 'Let her be at home; oh, please let her be at home!' When he reached the house and opened the door his hand was shaking.

There stood Mrs Pepperpot, quite her normal size and with no sign of a broomstick. She was decorating his birthday cake and on the table, neatly laid on a little cloth, was the precious pipe with its silver band.

'Many Happy Returns of the Day!' said Mrs Pepperpot. 'Come and have your meal now. Then you can put

on a clean shirt and take your wife to dance all night at the bonfire party!'

'Anything you say!' said Mr Pepperpot; he was so relieved she hadn't gone off with the witches of Mid-summer's Eve.

Mrs Pepperpot's Birthday

IT WAS Mrs Pepperpot's birthday, so she had asked her neighbours in to coffee at three o'clock. All day she had been scrubbing and polishing, and now it was ten minutes to three and she was putting the final touches to the strawberry layer cake on the kitchen table. As she stood balancing the last strawberry on a spoon, she suddenly felt herself shrinking, not slowly as she sometimes did, but so fast that she didn't even have time to put the strawberry on a plate. It rolled on to the floor and Mrs Pepperpot tumbled after it. But she quickly picked herself up and jumped into the cat's basket. Puss was a bit surprised, but allowed her to snuggle down with the kittens. In her black-and-white-striped skirt and white blouse, she hoped the guests would take her for one of the cat-family, until the magic wore off and she could be her real size again. For you may remember that Mrs Pepperpot never liked anyone to see her when she was tiny.

There was a knock at the door, and, when it wasn't

answered, Sarah from South Farm walked into the little front hall, carrying a huge bunch of lilac.

'Many Happy Returns of the Day!' said Sarah. There was no reply, so she peered into the kitchen, thinking Mrs Pepperpot might be in there, though, naturally, she didn't look in the cat-basket. Somehow she managed to knock over the flower-vase on the hall table, and the water spilled on the tablecloth and on to the floor.

'Oh dear, oh dear!' thought Sarah. 'I shall have to mop that up before anybody notices.'

But at that moment there was another knock at the

door. So Sarah ran into the kitchen and hid in a cupboard.

In came Norah from North Farm, and she was carrying a very nice tablecloth.

'Many Happy Returns!' she said, but, as she got no answer, she looked round for Mrs Pepperpot, and her parcel swept the vase off the table on to the floor.

'That's bad!' thought Norah. 'I must put it back before anybody comes.'

But before she could do it there was another knock on the door and Norah hurried into the bedroom and crept under the bed.

Esther from East Farm came in, carrying a handsome glass bowl for Mrs Pepperpot. When she had said 'Many Happy Returns!' and no one answered, she walked

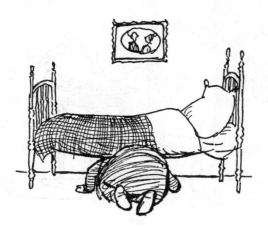

straight into the living-room. Carrying the bowl in front of her, she didn't notice the vase on the floor and put her foot straight on it. There was a nasty crunch and there it lay, in smithereens!

'Goodness gracious, what have I done?' thought Esther. 'Perhaps if I hide behind this curtain no one will know who did it!' So she quickly wrapped herself in one of the curtains.

At that moment the clock struck three, and the magic wore off; there was Mrs Pepperpot as large as life, walking through the kitchen. 'Coo-ee!' she called. 'You can all come out now!'

So Sarah stepped out of the cupboard, Norah crawled from under the bed, while Esther unwrapped herself from the curtain in the living-room.

At first they looked a bit sheepish, but then they said 'Many Happy Returns!' all over again and they had a good laugh, while Mrs Pepperpot swept up the broken vase, threw away the dead flowers and put the wet tablecloth in the wash-tub.

Then she thanked them for their fine presents; the table was spread with Norah's tablecloth, Esther's glass bowl was filled with fresh water, and the huge bunch of lilac that Sarah had brought was put into it.

After that Mrs Pepperpot brought in the coffee and

cakes and they all sat down to enjoy themselves. But on the strawberry layer cake there was one strawberry missing.

'You see,' said Mrs Pepperpot, when they asked her what had happened to it, 'my *first* visitor this afternoon was the little old woman who shrinks, and she was so tiny today that one strawberry was all she could manage to eat. So I gave her that and a thimble of milk to wash it down.'

'Didn't you ask her to stay, so that we could see her?' asked Sarah, for they were all very curious about the little old woman who shrank, and nobody thereabouts had ever seen her.

'She was sorry, she said, but she was in a tearing hurry; she had some business with a mouse, her night watchman or something. But she told me to tell you she did enjoy our little game of hide-and-seek!'

Mrs Pepperpot Turns Fortune-Teller

EVERY MORNING when Mr Pepperpot goes off to work Mrs Pepperpot stands at the window and watches him till he disappears round the bend to the main road. Then

she settles down in the chair by the kitchen table, picks up her empty coffee cup and starts reading her fortune in it.

Now you probably didn't know that Mrs Pepperpot could read fortunes in a cup. Well, she can; she can tell from the way the coffee grounds lie what road she will take that day and whether she will meet joy or sorrow before nightfall. Sometimes she sees the shape of a heart in the cup and that means she will have a new sweetheart. But that makes Mrs Pepperpot laugh, for to her it means she will probably get a new pet to look after— perhaps a poor little bird with a broken wing or a stray kitten on her doorstep, getting tamer and tamer as it laps up the food and milk she gives it.

But if the grounds form a cross she knows she must watch her step, for that means she will break something; it could be when she is washing up or when she is scrubbing the floor. If she sees a clear drop of coffee running down the side of the cup that means she will hurt herself in some way and will need not only a bandage but maybe a doctor as well. And so it goes on; there are many more signs that she can read, but she only does it for herself, never for other people, even if they ask her. It's just an amusement, she says, something to while away the time when she is at home alone all day.

Well, this day—it was a Friday too—Mrs Pepperpot had planned to give the house a good clean out and then she was going to bake a cake for Mr Pepperpot. Apart from that she was just going to take it easy for a change. So, when she had watched her husband turn the corner, she picked up their two coffee cups and was just about to put them in the sink. But then she stopped herself.

'There, what am I doing? I nearly forgot to have a look at my fortune for today!' So she took one of the cups back to the table and sat down. 'Let's see, now,' she said and turned the cup round and round in her hand. 'Oh dear, oh dear!' she exclaimed, 'what's this I see? A big cross? I shall have to mind how I go today and no mistake!'

At that very moment she shrank, and in no time at all she was no bigger than the coffee cup and both she and the cup fell off the chair on to the floor.

'That was a bit of a come-down!' she said, and felt both her arms and her legs to see if there were any bones broken. But when she found she was still all in one piece she lay still for a moment, not daring to look at the cup. For it was one of her best ones, and she was sure it must have been broken by the fall.

At last she said to herself, 'I suppose I shall have to have a look.' And when she did she found to her

great surprise that the cup was not even cracked or chipped.

But she was still worried. 'If that isn't it there'll be something else for me to break today,' she said miserably as she squatted down to look into the cup, for it was lying on its side.

'Oh me, oh my!' she cried. 'If this isn't my unlucky day!' She had caught sight of a large clear drop on the side of the cup. 'This means tears, but I wonder what will make me cry?'

Suddenly there was a loud BANG! inside the kitchen cupboard. Mrs Pepperpot nearly jumped out of her skin with fright.

'There! Now isn't that just like Mr P., setting a mouse-trap in the cupboard, although he knows it's not necessary now that I have a mouse for a night watchman. It's only now and again that a baby mouse gets into the cupboard by mistake—before he's learned the mouse rules. It's not as if they *mean* to do any damage, so it's silly to take any notice. I wonder if I dare open the door a little to see what's happened? I suppose I'd better; the little thing might just have caught its tail and I could free it. But, of course, it might be worse than that; the cup said tears, and tears it will be, no doubt!'

So Mrs Pepperpot went over to the cupboard and pulled gently at the door. But she closed her eyes to keep back the tears which were ready to come at any moment. When she had the door opened enough to look in she opened first one eye, then the other, and then she flopped down on the floor, clapping her hands on her knees, and burst out laughing.

Right enough, the trap had snapped, but there was nothing in it. Instead two baby mice were happily playing just beside it with two empty cotton-reels. Mrs Pepperpot thought it was the funniest sight she'd ever seen.

'Hullo, Mrs Pepperpot!' squealed one of the baby mice. 'Have you shrunk again?'

'We hoped you would!' said the other one, ' 'cos my brother and I had never seen you small before, and

167

Granny said we could come in here and have a peep—
just in case you shrunk. We weren't being naughty—just
playing cars—and then we bumped into that nasty thing
which went snap over there.'

'Will you play with us?' asked the first little mouse.
'You sit in the car and we'll pull you along.'

And when Mrs Pepperpot looked closer she saw that
the baby mice had fixed a matchbox over the cotton-reels
and the whole contraption really moved.

'Let's go!' shouted Mrs Pepperpot, and jumped into
the box.

So they played at cars, taking turns to sit in the
matchbox, and Mrs Pepperpot laughed while the baby
mice squealed with delight, till, all of a sudden, they
heard a scratching sound above them.

'That's enough, children!' called granny mouse,

whose head had appeared in a hole in the back wall. 'The cat's on top of the cupboard and the door is open!'

Before you could say 'knife' the two baby mice had disappeared through the hole, squeaking 'Thanks for the game!' as they went.

'Thank you!' said Mrs Pepperpot, and stepped out of the cupboard to see what that cat was up to.

There she was, standing on top of the cupboard waving her tail expectantly when Mrs Pepperpot came out. But Mrs Pepperpot was not standing any nonsense; she shouted at the cat: 'What are you doing up there? You get down at once or I'll teach you a lesson as soon as I grow again! Maybe it's you who are going to break something for me today? Yes, I can feel it in my bones. I know if I have another look in that cup there'll be more calamity there for me.'

By now she was just as worked up as she had been before her little game with the mice. But she couldn't resist having another look in the cup. 'Goodness gracious!' she cried. 'It's just as I thought, doctor and bandages, ambulances and everything! As if I hadn't trouble enough already! Down you get, cat, and make it quick!'

'All right! Keep your hair on,' said the cat. 'I was only doing my duty when I heard a suspicious noise in the cupboard. I'm coming down now.'

'Mind how you go! Be careful! I don't want anything broken. I'll stand here below and direct you,' said Mrs Pepperpot.

'Anybody would think I'd never jumped off a cupboard before, and I'm not in the habit of breaking things,' answered the cat, as he made his way gingerly past a big china bowl. But just on the edge of the cupboard lay a large pair of scissors, and neither the cat nor Mrs Pepperpot had seen them.

Mrs Pepperpot was busy with her warnings: 'Mind that bowl!' she shouted, standing right beneath those scissors.

The cat was being as careful as she could, but her tail brushed against the scissors, sending them flying, point downwards, to the floor. There they stood quivering!

Mrs Pepperpot had just managed to jump out of the way, but now she was too frightened to move. 'So that was it!' she stammered at last. She felt herself all over again, for this time she was *sure* she must be hurt. But she couldn't find as much as a scratch!

A moment later she was her normal size. So she pulled the scissors out of the floor and lifted the cat down out of harm's way. Then she set to work cleaning the house and just had time to bake her cake before she heard her husband at the door.

But what a state he was in! The tears were pouring out of his eyes because of the bitter wind outside, and anyway he had a bad cold. One hand he was holding behind his back: he had fallen off his bicycle, had broken his cycle lamp and cut his hand on the glass!

As she hurriedly searched for something to tie round his hand, Mrs Pepperpot thought how odd it was that it was Mr Pepperpot who had tears in his eyes; it was Mr Pepperpot that had broken something, and had hurt himself so that he had to have a bandage on. Very odd indeed!

But if you think this cured Mrs Pepperpot of reading her fortune in a coffee cup you are very much mistaken. The only thing is, she *does* take more care not to pick up the wrong cup and read her husband's fortune instead of her own.

The New Year's Eve Adventure

It happened every New Year's Eve. Mrs Pepperpot would say to herself: 'This year I really will watch the fireworks and listen to the church bells ringing in the New Year.'

Mr Pepperpot said the same. They would dress up in their best clothes, and sit down to a meal of boiled bacon and dumplings, followed by Mrs Pepperpot's special little cakes with cloudberry jam and whipped cream. Afterwards they would each sit in their favourite chair and read the magazines they had got for Christmas.

The only sound was the ticking of the clock; tick, tock, tick, tock. . . .

After a while Mrs Pepperpot would begin to feel sleepy, so she got up and made some coffee. When they had drunk the coffee, Mr Pepperpot would walk to the window to see if there were any rockets going off.

So the hours went by and when the clock finally struck twelve and the rockets shot up in great arches through the sky and the bell-ringer started pulling the rope in the bell-tower, well . . . you've guessed it . . . Mr and Mrs Pepperpot would be fast asleep in their chairs and never hear a thing.

So this year they decided not to bother to stay up, but just go to bed at their usual hour. When they had eaten their supper and drunk their coffee they sat reading their magazines till they got sleepy. First Mr Pepperpot started stretching and yawning.

'I think I'll turn in,' he muttered.

'You do that,' said Mrs Pepperpot, who had been looking at the same page of her magazine for the last twenty minutes. 'I'll just let the cat out. Come on, Pussy,' she called, 'you're going out in the snow.'

She followed the cat on to the doorstep and looked up at the moon to see if there was a ring round it.

Just at that moment she SHRANK!

If you've met Mrs Pepperpot before, you will know that she has this unfortunate habit of turning small – just the size of a pepperpot – at the most inconvenient times.

'Goodness Gracious!' she cried as she rolled over in the snow.

'What a bit of luck!' said the cat, 'Now you can come along with me and see something no human has ever seen. Jump on my back!'

That's another thing that happens when Mrs Pepperpot turns small; she can understand animal language and they can understand her.

'Well, if it's really special . . .' said Mrs Pepperpot, climbing on to Pussy's back, 'but I must be back home when they ring the New Year in.'

The cat set off with Mrs Pepperpot on her back. It was

very dark and the wind was blowing snow in her face, but she could tell they were going up the side of the mountain. Through the trees she could hear the sound of heavy feet and crashing branches, and as the moon came out from behind the clouds, she could see it was a big bull moose with his family behind him. In the tree-tops she could hear the squirrel chattering and above her head came the whirring sound of grouse wings. There was an owl hooting and a fox barking, and she could see the darting shapes of hares as they zig-zagged across the snow or ran round in a ring. But they were all going the same way and at last they stopped in front of a huge rock-face.

'What are they all stopping for?' whispered Mrs Pepperpot, putting her mouth very close to the cat's ear.

'They're listening; don't you hear it yourself?' answered the cat.

Mrs Pepperpot listened and after a moment she *did* hear something; it sounded like the faint rumble of a motorbike, very far away.

'That's him all right, snoring!' said the cat.

'Will you please explain?' Mrs Pepperpot said. She was getting tired of all this mystery.

'Well,' said the cat, 'behind that rock is the winter lair of the king of the forest, the big brown bear. He's been sleeping in there for several months now, but on New Year's Eve he has to turn over on his other side.'

'What happens if he doesn't turn over?' asked Mrs Pepperpot.

'Oh, it's terrible!' said the cat, 'if he lies on the same side all the winter, you see, he wakes up in the Spring in a very bad mood, all stiff and sore. Then he takes it out on the rest of us and woe betide any animal that gets in his way!'

'Well,' said Mrs Pepperpot, 'how d'you get him to turn over?'

'We make all the noise we can, but it's getting more and more difficult each year, as the King is getting older and deafer. We had a real job rousing him last year,' said the cat.

None of the other animals had said anything up to now, they were all so busy getting their breath back. But now one of the hares, gleaming in his white winter coat, spoke up:

'What we need is a new sort of noise – much sharper

than all this yowling of foxes, and tooting of owls – a bit of dynamite would be good, like the men use when they're blasting holes in the rocks.'

Mrs Pepperpot snapped her fingers: 'That gives me an idea! I have just what we need at home. But I shall need some help,' Mrs Pepperpot was thinking hard as she spoke.

The bull moose was standing close by. He looked as big as a house from down there, but she cupped her hands and shouted up to him:

'Hi, Moose! Can you carry me back to my house? I want to fetch my box of tricks.'

The moose at once knelt down in the snow, so that Mrs Pepperpot could climb on to his head, where she settled herself between his antlers.

'Right, let's go!' she shouted.

In no time at all the moose had run down the mountain to the valley and then up the hill to Mrs Pepperpot's house.

'You'll have to be very quiet,' said Mrs Pepperpot as the moose knelt down to let her slide off his neck. 'We don't want to scare my husband.'

Luckily the door to the outhouse was open, and there were no dogs or cats or hens in there to raise the alarm. Mrs Pepperpot went straight over to a large carton covered in paper and carefully tied with string.

'In this box there are enough bangs to wake a cartload of bears,' she told the moose, who was standing quietly in the doorway.

Over the years Mrs Pepperpot had bought firecrackers

and rockets and roman candles and so on to let off on New Year's Eve, but as they were never used, she had quite a big collection.

Now the problem was how to get the box hitched onto the moose, so that he could drag it back up the mountain to the bear's lair. Mrs Pepperpot got him to kneel down again, then she fastened a rope first round the carton and then round the moose's antlers. Then she swung herself back into her 'saddle' on his nobbly forehead, and away they went down the hill, the carton lurching along like a crazy toboggan.

'I hope the fireworks don't blow up on the way,' thought Mrs Pepperpot, but she said nothing to the moose, who was carefully avoiding the trees as they climbed up the mountain. Luckily the snow was thick enough to make a smooth path for the box, which was not very heavy.

The birds and the animals were all waiting for them when they arrived.

'Come on, everybody!' shouted Mrs Pepperpot as she jumped down into the snow, 'help me get the string and the paper off.'

The owl and the grouse pecked away at the string, and the foxes used their sharp claws to tear off the paper. At last Mrs Pepperpot could open the box.

'There you are, children,' she said, 'every kind of banger and firecracker you can think of. If His Majesty King Bear doesn't wake up when this lot goes off, you can take it from me he's dead!'

'How will you light them?' asked the white-coated hare who had suggested dynamite.

'Good question!' said Mrs Pepperpot, 'but luckily I had a box of matches in my apron pocket when I turned small.'

But first she told all the birds and animals to stand well out of the way. All except her faithful friend, the squirrel, who had helped her many times before. Sitting on his back, she told him to climb a few feet up a tall pine tree near the box. From there she struck all the matches at once and threw them into the box.

'Now shin up to the top as fast as you can,' she shouted, as the first bangers started going off. The squirrel kept to the far side of the tree-trunk, and when he got to the top he took a flying leap to the next tree, where they landed safely and well out of reach of any flying missiles.

'Phew! That was a near thing!' gasped Mrs Pepperpot, who had been more frightened by the squirrel's aerobatics than the hissing and popping that was going on below.

Looking down from so high, it really was a spectacular show, as the whole box of fireworks went up in one colossal din and blaze. It lit up the snow, the trees, the sky and the animals and birds scattering in every direction.

As the last bangers fizzled out and the sky grew dark again, Mrs Pepperpot heard a very different sound, and so did all the animals and birds; it was like the creaking of a heavy door followed by a long, loud 'Yaaaaaawn!'

'Hooray!' shouted all the animals and the birds squawked excitedly; 'King Bear has turned! King Bear has turned!'

The squirrel carried Mrs Pepperpot down to the ground and she found herself surrounded by stamping feet and flapping wings; everyone wanted to thank her.

'Help, help!' she cried, 'you're smothering me!'

But the next moment she was back to her normal size, standing in the snow by the big rock face.

Every bird, every animal had vanished in the darkness

– except one. Mrs Pepperpot felt warm fur rubbing against her leg.

'Is that you, Pussy?' she said, picking up the purring cat. 'Well, you certainly gave me a New Year adventure this year!'

And as she trudged back home through the snow, the church bells began to ring out and beautiful rockets lit up the sky over the village.

Fate and Mrs Pepperpot

Mrs Pepperpot is fond of fortune-telling, but she only does it for herself, never for other people. When she has finished a cup of coffee, she likes to peer at the grounds at the bottom of the cup to see what fortune has in store for her.

This was what she was doing one cold morning in January. 'My goodness!' she exclaimed excitedly. 'I can see a long journey over water! I knew my luck would change. Now all I have to do is pack my bag and wait for it to happen.'

She was just about to go up to the attic for her old suit-case, when she remembered that she had dipped her biscuit in the coffee, so there were biscuit crumbs mixed with the grounds and that didn't count.

'Ah well,' she sighed, 'I suppose I couldn't really expect it. And what would Mr Pepperpot do if I went off by my-self on a holiday in the middle of winter?'

She picked up the magazine that was lying on the table. It was open at the page headed 'The Stars and You'. She looked under Taurus, for her birthday was in May. It said: 'Prepare for a journey over water.'

This was astonishing!

'It *must* be fate!' said Mrs Pepperpot. 'This time there's no denying it. I will pack at once.'

Then she glanced at the date of the magazine; it was a year old!

'I might have known it,' she said disgustedly, as she threw the paper into the stove. 'Anyway, who wants to go trapesing off to the South of France or wherever. I'm all right here, aren't I? Got my husband and my house to look after and my cat. . . .' She got up and started bustling about, sweeping the floor, cleaning out the sink and peeling the potatoes for supper. But just as she was standing there, she suddenly felt a tingling in the sole of her right foot. She waited for a moment; yet, it was quite definitely tingling!

'That settles it,' she said firmly to herself, as she went up to the attic to fetch her suitcase.

Tingling under your right foot, you see, is another sign that you are going on a journey, and this time Mrs Pepperpot was quite sure there was no mistake.

She came down with the battered old suitcase. 'Long time since you've had an airing,' she said, looking at it ruefully. 'Never mind. Next thing is to wash all my clothes to be ready for the trip.'

But she found she had no wash-powder, so she put on her hat and coat and a warm muffler and set out for the shop.

The shop was full of customers. At the door stood a lady with a handful of brochures. She was advertising a new wash-powder.

'This product is not like any you have used before,' she was saying, 'it will take all the work out of washing-day.'

'Can't fool me with that sort of nonsense,' muttered Mrs Pepperpot. But the lady went on: 'In every packet you buy today there is a numbered coupon, and one of those has a lucky number. Whoever gets the lucky number will win a seven-day sunshine holiday for two at beautiful Las Palmas in the Canary Islands. Don't miss this chance, ladies and gentlemen, the lucky number will be drawn tonight and displayed in the shop-window at closing time.'

She hadn't finished speaking before everyone started grabbing the packets of wash-powder. Some bought as many as six!

'Take them all year to get through that lot,' muttered Mrs Pepperpot. She just bought one packet.

'That's all I need for *my* lucky number,' she said as she trudged home through the snow. She was just wondering whom she should invite to go with her on her sun-shine holiday, Mrs North, perhaps, or Mrs West, when whoops! her feet slid from under her and she SHRANK!

She had been walking on the path where the snow was soft and not too slippery, but now both she and the packet tumbled on to the glass-hard surface of the road, just where it sloped steeply down towards the stream.

'Oh me, oh my!' she moaned, as she started to slide after the packet. 'This is a journey all right, but not quite what I intended.'

Faster and faster they went, till wham! The packet struck a tree-stump just be the edge of the stream. Mrs Pepperpot landed on top of the packet and the force of it pushed them both into the icy water!

Off they went again, whirling and bobbing in the fast-flowing stream, Mrs Pepperpot clinging on as best she could.

'Skipper of my own yacht on a luxury cruise!' she joked, but she didn't feel very cheerful. 'Not much hope of rescue here, I'm afraid.'

'Caw, caw!' croaked a voice from above. 'Don't say that!'

And before she had time to see who was there, she had been picked up by her skirt and set down again on the bank of the stream.

Mrs Pepperpot blinked at her rescuer, a big black crow.

'Thanks, pal, that wasn't a minute too soon! But could you please hurry after my packet and rescue that too?'

'Caw, caw! Right you are!' cried the crow, swooping

and darting after the swirling packet till he could get a hold on it with his beak.

With some difficulty he hauled it to the bank where Mrs Pepperpot stood ready to help pull it out of the water.

'I'm afraid your wash-powder will be a bit soggy by now,' said the crow, when they had got it safely on land.

'Never mind,' said Mrs Pepperpot, 'thanks to you, I can still believe in my lucky day.'

'Anything to oblige, Mrs P. Many's the nice piece of bacon rind I've had at your back door. Glad to get a chance to do you a good turn.'

There the conversation came to an end, because Mrs Pepperpot grew to her normal size and the crow flew off. But she waved to him as she hurried home with her wet packet under her arm.

Indoors she emptied the packet into a bowl, carefully taking out the coupon which she put to dry on a towel. She noted the number: 347

'That's good,' she said, 'it has a seven in it. Sure to be a winner.'

Then she set to with her washing and she worked so hard, she never noticed the time, till she heard Mr Pepperpot open the front door.

'Hallo, my love!' he shouted, 'you'll never guess my luck!'

Mrs Pepperpot stared at him; in one hand he held a packet of the same wash-powder she had bought, and in the other a coupon!

'Let me tell you!' went on Mr Pepperpot excitedly. 'I went to the shop this morning on my way to work to get some baccy, and there was this lady. . . .'

'I know,' said Mrs Pepperpot, 'I saw her too.'

'You did? Well, of course I bought a packet of her wash-powder – come in handy, I thought, and you never know – stand as good a chance as anyone else. . . .'

Mrs Pepperpot couldn't bear the suspense any longer: 'Come to the point, man!'

'All right, all right! I just went back to look at the number in the window and it's the same as mine! 693.'

Mrs Pepperpot turned her head away.

'Congratulations,' she said. 'I hope you have a very nice trip.'

'Well!' said her husband, 'you don't sound very en-thusiastic. Don't you want to go on a sunshine holiday to the Canary Islands?'

'But . . . but . . .' stammered Mrs Pepperpot. 'How was I to know you'd be taking *me*?'

'You silly old thing – who else?' laughed Mr Pepperpot and gave her a smacking kiss.

Mrs Pepperpot Helps Arne

Mr and Mrs Pepperpot *did* enjoy their holidays in the Canaries and Mrs Pepperpot never shrank the whole time they were there. They bathed in the sea and got brown lying in the sun and in the evenings they listened to the music in the restaurant and tried the strange food they were served.

But at the end of the seven days they were quite glad to go home to Norway with all its ice and snow. It was nice, too, to get back to their own little house on the hill, and to sit down to their favourite supper of fried herring and boiled potatoes, followed by pancakes and bilberry jam.

'They can keep their foreign la-di-da meals,' said Mr Pepperpot, 'my wife's cooking is good enough for me!'

'I'll remember that next time you grumble!' said Mrs Pepperpot.

So the wintry days went on and soon it was time for the school-children to have their half-term holiday. Most of them were keen skiers and this meant they could ski all day every day for a whole week!

Mrs Pepperpot could hear them shouting and laughing as they rushed down the slopes near her house.

But one day when she was baking bread in the kitchen,

she looked out of the window and saw a little boy making his way slowly and carefully down the road below. He looked very unsteady on his skis.

Mrs Pepperpot opened the window and called to him:

'Hi there! Come up here a minute.'

The little fellow took off his skis and climbed up the hill. Mrs Pepperpot met him in the door.

'D'you like fresh-baked bread with butter and honey on it?' she asked.

'Oh yes, please,' said the boy.

'Well, come on in and sit down. I'll have a cup of coffee at the same time.'

While he munched the bread and honey, Mrs Pepperpot asked him his name.

'Arne,' he said.

'Why weren't you up on the slope, ski-ing with the others, Arne?' she asked.

''Cos I'm not very good at it,' said Arne, looking at her sadly, 'and the others tease me and call me a cowardy custard. They say I'm afraid of the moose up there in the pine trees and a lot of other stuff. They don't like me!'

He wiped a hand over his eyes and gave a little sniff.

'Don't you worry, Arne,' said Mrs Pepperpot, 'I won't call you a coward,' and she put an arm round his shoulders.

'This is my first winter in the snow. Before that, I lived in France with my mum and dad.'

'No wonder you're new to ski-ing then!' said Mrs Pepperpot. 'D'you know, when I was a little girl I was very afraid to go down those steep slopes. But I found a way to get over it.'

Arne was looking at her eagerly now: 'What did you do?'

'You'll laugh when you hear,' said Mrs Pepperpot. 'I took my mother's old dough trough – the very same one I've been using today to make the bread. Look, it's got nice high sides to stop you falling out, and I took it up to the top of that slope and rode down in it. In fact, it was such fun I wouldn't mind doing it again.'

'Weren't you frightened after that?'

'Never again,' said Mrs Pepperpot. 'If you like, we could try it together, because I have another trough as well.'

Arne looked doubtful.

'I don't know – people might see us. . . .'

'Not if we get up very early in the morning and go up to the top before anyone else is about.'

So Arne agreed and next day, when the sun rose, he and Mrs Pepperpot set off, each with a dough trough under their arm. They walked right to the top of the higher slope, where the row of pine trees cast a shadow on the hard glistening snow.

'I hope no one saw us,' said Arne, who kept looking back over his shoulder.

'Of course not,' said Mrs Pepperpot, 'all those big boys will be snoring their heads off at this time of day.'

But Arne was still nervous: 'Have you ever seen a moose come out of those trees?'

'Bless you, yes, but he knows me, and he won't bother us, I promise you,' said Mrs Pepperpot.

'I think I'll go first!' said Arne, as he settled himself in the dough trough.

'Off you go, then!' said Mrs Pepperpot and gave him a good push to start him off.

Arne shot down the slope. The wooden trough churned up the snow; it blew in his eyes, so that he had to close them, and he couldn't see where he was going. But he didn't mind, because there were no obstacles in the way and he was holding onto the sides very tightly. In fact, he was really enjoying the ride. That is, till the trough stopped and he opened his eyes.

There, on either side of him, stood the whole crowd of boys from his class!

'Here comes the champion tobogganer!' shouted one, and they all roared with laughter.

'The very latest design!' jeered another.

'What did you do with the old woman? Isn't she coming down in her trough too? Or perhaps she's even more scared than you are. . . .'

And so they went on, while poor Arne wished he could bury himself in the snow and that Mrs Pepperpot would not appear.

From the top of the slope Mrs Pepperpot had seen the boys arrive. She was just wondering what to do, when she SHRANK!

For once she was not too sorry to be tiny. At least the

boys wouldn't see her. She would just sit in her trough and wait till they went away.

But at that moment the bull moose came ambling out of the pine trees. 'Hi, Moose!' shouted Mrs Pepperpot from the trough.

The big animal came over and blew hot air on Mrs Pepperpot through his huge nostrils: 'What's the trouble this time, Mrs Pepperpot?' he asked.

'Well,' she said, 'I've had an idea, and if you'll help me today, maybe I can do you a good turn another time.

'Ho, ho,' he chuckled, 'what could a little lady like you do for me?'

'You'll be surprised,' she answered, and then she told him her plan: he was to sit in the big trough and slide down the slope to where the group of boys were standing. The last part of the plan she whispered in his ear, and then she gave him a good push and away he went.

Well, that big bull moose had the greatest difficulty in keeping his balance in the wooden trough, but he managed not to fall off till it came to a standstill at the place where the boys stood – or rather *had* stood. For they had seen him coming and had scattered in every direction as fast as they could go.

All except poor Arne, who was standing there with his trough. His eyes were filled with tears, so he didn't see anything till the moose came to rest right next to him.

As the huge beast got to his feet, Arne was too frightened to move. But the moose took a step towards him and then did something which made all the boys stare: with his big thick tongue he licked Arne's face!

Arne was no longer frightened; he could tell the moose was friendly. He put his hand up to the big head and stroked his ears. Then the moose quietly ambled back to the slope and disappeared in the trees.

And Mrs Pepperpot? Well, she appeared on the scene, as large as life, just as those boys came edging up to shake Arne by the hand.

'He's a brave boy, isn't he?' she said, putting her arm round Arne's shoulder; 'who'd have thought such a little fellow could tame that old bull moose?'

Spring Cleaning

It was a beautiful day in March. The sun was doing its best to melt the last remaining snow-drifts and cast a glow over the tall pine trees on the mountain ridge. Everything suddenly looked sharper and clearer in outline. Even the wooden walls of Mrs Pepperpot's house seemed to shine like polished tin. But when she looked at her windows she didn't thank the sun; it showed up how very dirty they were.

'Oh dear,' she said to herself. 'I can see it's time for spring-cleaning again. Well, I might as well get down to it straight away, I suppose.'

She went into the kitchen to get out her bucket, her scrubbing brush and plenty of soap and scouring powder. Mrs Pepperpot was pretty thorough when she got going – in fact, she enjoyed spring-cleaning.

She was just about to start on the windows when she heard a slow buzzing sound over by the stove. A big black fly had come out of the corner where it had been sleeping.

'Oho!' she said, 'So the sun's woken you up too, has it? Well, you needn't think I'm letting you lay eggs all over my house, making millions of flies to blacken my windows in the summer. I'll fix you!' and she rushed at the fly with a fly-swatter.

But the fly got away, because at that moment Mrs Pepperpot SHRANK!

'You wait!' she shrilled in her tiny voice, as she rolled along the floor, 'I'll get you!'

'Don't worry,' said a voice from the corner.

Mrs Pepperpot turned round; it was a large spider hanging by its thread from a web it had spun between the grandfather clock and the wall.

'Don't worry,' said the spider, 'I'll deal with that pest.'

'You gave me quite a fright!' said Mrs Pepperpot, 'I don't mean to be rude, but I've never seen you so close to before, and I didn't know you were so hairy and ugly. . . .'

'I could return the compliment,' said the spider, 'but on the whole you look a bit better when you're small than when you're tramping round the kitchen in your great big shoes. Anyway, did you hear me offer to catch that fat fly for you?'

'Yes, I did,' answered Mrs Pepperpot, 'but I certainly wouldn't let you roll that poor creature up in your horrible web to be eaten for breakfast. No, indeed. If I had seen that contraption of yours before I shrank, I would have whisked it away with my broom!'

'Leave it to me!' said another little voice right behind her. This time it was a mouse.

'It's you, is it? And what d'you think a little scrap like you can do?' asked Mrs Pepperpot scornfully.

'Who's talking?' squeaked the mouse cheekily, 'you're not exactly outsize yourself at the moment. At least *I* can run up the clock – dickory, dickory dock!' he laughed. 'And then I can snip that web with my sharp teeth as easy as winking!'

'I'm sure you can,' said Mrs Pepperpot, 'but don't you see? That web is the spider's livelihood. Without those threads she couldn't catch her food and she would die.'

'Well, in that case,' said the mouse, 'I suppose you're supplying me with *my* livelihood when you leave the cover off the cheese dish in the larder, hee, hee!'

'You little thief!' shouted Mrs Pepperpot, shaking her tiny fist at the mouse. 'You push it off yourself, you and your wretched family. But I'll set a trap for you this very evening!'

'Did I hear a mouse?' asked another voice from the door. It was the cat. 'Where is it? I'm just ready for my dinner.'

'No, no!' shrieked Mrs Pepperpot, waving her arms at the cat, while the mouse was trying to hide behind her skirt. 'You leave the mouse alone, you great brute, you. He hasn't done you any harm, has he?'

'Woof! Woof! Who's a brute round here?' The head of a strange dog was peering round the door. When he caught sight of the cat he darted after her, knocking Mrs Pepperpot over as he ran round the table.

The cat managed to get out of the door with the dog close behind her when, luckily, at that moment Mrs Pepperpot grew to her normal size! She lost no time in throwing a stick at the dog while Pussy jumped on to the shed roof. The dog went on barking till Mrs Pepperpot gave him a bone. Then he trotted off down the hill.

'Dear me, what a to-do!' thought Mrs Pepperpot, 'But

it makes you wonder; every little creature is hunted by a bigger creature who in turn is hunted by a bigger one. Where does it all end?'

'Right here!' said a deep voice behind her.

Mrs Pepperpot nearly jumped out of her skin, but when she turned round it was her husband standing there.

'Oh,' she said, 'I thought you were an ogre come to gobble me up!'

'Well!' said Mr Pepperpot, 'Is that all the thanks I get for coming home early to help with the spring-cleaning?'

'You darling man!' said Mrs Pepperpot, giving him a great big kiss.

Easter Chicks

Every year when it gets near Easter time and the shop windows are full of fluffy cotton wool Easter chicks, Mrs Pepperpot sends a message to the children round about that she would like them to do her shopping for her. The children are only too pleased, because Mrs Pepperpot always gives them sweets, and sometimes even money to spend on themselves. So there is often quite a queue outside her door. But as soon as Easter is over and those yellow chicks disappear from the window displays, Mrs Pepperpot starts to do her shopping herself again.

Now why does the little old woman behave in this peculiar way? I'll tell you.

One Easter, many years ago, Mrs Pepperpot got it into her head that she wanted to rear chickens. She could have bought day-old chicks from a hatchery, but no:

'Chickens need a mother!' she declared.

So she went to a neighbour and borrowed a broody hen. Not all hens want to rear chicks; some spend their time preening their feathers, looking for food and laying their eggs wherever a box is handy. But a broody hen starts to collect her eggs in one nest and gets all hot and bothered if anyone tries to take them away.

The neighbour put the whole nest with ten eggs in a carton and the broody hen on top, and Mrs Pepperpot carried it home very carefully. She had already prepared a corner of her sitting-room with a little curtain across to keep out the draught, and the hen settled down very nicely.

Mr Pepperpot was not pleased: 'Proper place for a hen is in the out-house,' he said. But every time he went near the broody hen to take her out, she pecked and squawked so much, he had to give it up.

Every day Mrs Pepperpot lifted the curtain and peeped in to see if the hen was all right. She brought her water and some grain, but the hen was not very interested in eating or drinking. She just sat there, keeping the eggs warm.

The day came when the hatching should begin.

Mrs Pepperpot walked round the house, singing. She was so excited, she couldn't keep still, and every so often she went over to the corner and crouched down to listen.

'Those little chicks should be pecking their way out of their shells any minute now,' she told herself.

And then she heard an unmistakable sound: 'Cheep, cheep!' it said, very faintly.

Immediately the mother hen started clucking and fussing. Soon there were more cheeps, until at last the mother hen strutted out from behind the curtain, followed by nine little golden chicks.

Mrs Pepperpot clapped her hands with joy as she watched them following their mother. Then she knelt down to see what had happened to the tenth egg.

It was still lying in the nest, quite smooth and whole among all the broken shells.

'Oh, you poor little thing,' said Mrs Pepperpot, 'Perhaps you need some help with that hard shell. . . .' But as she stretched out her hand to pick it up, she SHRANK!

She not only found herself lying in the nest by the egg, but there was a great shadow towering over her – Mother Hen!

'Don't peck me!' she cried, because the hen looked very fierce, 'I was only trying to help your last chick out of the egg.'

The hen opened her beak and squawked at her. It sounded something like: '*Fi fi, finicula!*'

'Now listen!' said Mrs Pepperpot, trying to dodge Mother Hen's flapping wings, 'I'm Mrs Pepperpot – you know – the old woman who shrinks, and I understand animal and bird language – but I don't know what you're talking about.'

The hen just went on squawking and gabbling her strange nonsense: '*Fi fi finicula, ratagusa balla tella!*'

'Will you listen a minute!' Mrs Pepperpot was losing patience; 'I'm not trying to hurt your chicks. You just take them for a nice walk round the room and leave me to sit here till I grow big again. Now, run along!'

The hen took no notice. She charged straight at Mrs

Pepperpot and with her strong wings buffeted her right out of the nest on to the mat where all the baby chicks were darting about and cheeping their heads off.

'What a din!' said Mrs Pepperpot, scrambling to her feet and trying to keep out of the way.

Mother Hen now turned her attention to her family. Clucking in a commanding tone, she chivvied them into line and made them follow behind her as she walked slowly across the room.

Mrs Pepperpot stood watching the wonderful way the chicks obeyed her, when suddenly Mother Hen turned round and saw her there.

'*Seguira linia malachita*' she squawked and rushed at her, pecking at Mrs Pepperpot's hair.

'Ouch!' shouted Mrs Pepperpot, 'What d'you think you're doing? I'm not one of your children!'

The only reply she got was more gibberish and more angry pecks. So, to avoid being pecked to pieces, she fell into line and followed Mother Hen till they came to the spot where Mrs Pepperpot had strewn some fine oatmeal for the baby chicks to eat.

Mother Hen stopped and clucked to the chicks to gather round. Then she showed them how to pick up the meal and soon they all had their heads down, their beaks sounding like tiny drums on the floor. Mrs Pepperpot had to laugh as she watched them, but not for long, because Mother Hen was after her again:

'*Mangiamello, mangiamello!*' and more pecks rained on the little old woman's head.

'Stop! Stop!' she yelled. 'I don't know what you're saying, but I'll have some oatmeal, if that's what you want.'

She picked some up in her hand and pretended to put it in her mouth.

'*Uccella stupida,*' scolded the hen, flapping her with a wing.

'Oh very well, you silly old fuss-pot!' said Mrs Pepperpot, and she got down on all fours and pretended to peck at the oatmeal with her nose.

When the baby chicks had had enough, Mother Hen led them over to a pan of water which Mrs Pepperpot had put there for them. Mother Hen showed them how to drink, dipping their beaks and then putting their heads well back.

'Drink like a hen? That's one thing you're not going to get me to do, madam!' declared Mrs Pepperpot.

'*Bere, bere!*' squawked the hen swooping on her so hard that she fell right into the pan of water.

The next moment she was back to her normal size and standing there with her wet clothes dripping on to the sitting-room floor.

'You're worse than my teacher at school!' said Mrs Pepperpot, rubbing her sore head.

The hen was now behaving very strangely, fluttering to and fro and calling anxiously.

'What's the matter?' said Mrs Pepperpot, 'looking for your lost chick?' and she went over to the nest and picked up the tenth egg. She broke the shell, but there was no chick inside.

'I'm afraid you'll have to do with nine,' she said, 'as I'm not following a hen around who doesn't even speak my language. Whoever heard of a bird that can't understand Mrs Pepperpot when she shrinks?'

'*Mi scusi!*' clucked the hen.

And suddenly Mrs Pepperpot understood what had happened. The hen was an Italian Leghorn and she was talking hen Italian!

The mystery was solved, and you would think Mrs Pepperpot would be satisfied. But she never got over the shock of having to be a baby chick and doing what she was told by Mother Hen.

So that's why she won't even look at those fluffy yellow Easter chicks in the shop window.

The Cuckoo

***

In May, when the first green veil of leaves cover the birch trees and the wagtail starts to follow the plough, that is the time for the cuckoo to arrive.

Mrs Pepperpot was just locking her door to go to the shop when she heard it:

'Cuckoo!'

'Cuckoo!' answered Mrs Pepperpot, but she didn't say it very loudly, in case the cuckoo might get annoyed. For Mrs Pepperpot is a little afraid of the cuckoo. It can bring good luck, but it can also bring you bad luck. It depends from which direction you hear it calling.

Mrs Pepperpot looked all around her, but couldn't see where the bird was sitting.

'Cuckoo!'

There it was again, and this time she was sure she heard it from the west.

' "Cuckoo from the west, all for the best!" ' she chanted, and went on her way down the hill, quite content. But soon she stopped, and a frightened look came over her face. What if her husband had heard the same bird? He would have heard it from the north, for he was working on the road down in the valley.

'Oh dear!' she said, ' "Cuckoo from the north, sorrow bring forth!" '

At that moment she SHRANK! and found herself sitting on the ground under a high pine tree. Up above she could hear the angry noise of her friend, the squirrel.

She called to him: 'Hi, squirrel! Could you come down here, please!'

'Chuck! Chuck!' he scolded, running down the tree trunk head first. 'What's up with Mrs Pepperpot this time? You look very woe-begone.'

'Well, its my husband, you see,' said Mrs Pepperpot, 'I'm afraid he'll have heard the cuckoo from the north, and that means bad luck for him.'

'Chuck! Just the sort of thing an old woman like you would worry about! What d'you want *me* to do about it?'

'I thought you might take me up to the top of the tree, so that I could talk to the cuckoo, and perhaps get him to call from the east. "Cuckoo from the East, harbingers a feast," you see.'

'Rubbish,' said the squirrel. 'But hurry up now. I've got better things to do than carry superstitious old women around!'

'So I notice!' said Mrs Pepperpot. 'There's egg-yolk round your nose.'

The squirrel's tail switched angrily. 'It's none of your business what I have for breakfast! Are you ready?' and he scuttled up to the top of the tall pine tree with Mrs Pepperpot.

Once up there, Mrs Pepperpot clung to a small branch. It made her giddy to look down.

'Bye, bye!' said the squirrel. 'I hope the cuckoo doesn't keep you waiting too long!'

'You're not going to leave me up here all alone, are you?' said poor Mrs Pepperpot.

'You silly woman! The cuckoo won't come near you if I'm here. I'll fetch you later.' And with that he was off.

Mrs Pepperpot's arms were quite stiff with holding on before the cuckoo finally alighted in the tree. He was a little surprised to find her there.

'Did you fall out of an aeroplane?' he asked.

'No, Mr Cuckoo,' said Mrs Pepperpot politely, 'I came up here to speak to you.'

'I'm a little busy just now . . .' said the cuckoo, opening his beak to call again.

'Stop, please!' cried Mrs Pepperpot.

The cuckoo shut his beak and looked at her in astonishment.

'Mr Cuckoo, will you do me a big favour?' she pleaded. 'Will you fly over to the east side of the valley and call from there?'

'Why should I?' said the cuckoo, 'I'm calling to my wife and she's on this side of the valley.'

'It'll bring good luck to my husband if you do. He's working down there on the road.'

The cuckoo looked flattered: 'Oh well, if you put it that way, of course I'll oblige.' And he flew off straight away.

A little while later Mrs Pepperpot heard him:

'Cuckoo!' he called and it sounded such a happy note, she was sure it would cheer her husband up.

Then she remembered she hadn't done her shopping yet, and Mr Pepperpot would be expecting a feast when he got home!

'Oh dear! Now what shall I do?' she wailed.

At that moment the squirrel reappeared.

'You moaning again?' he said. 'I'll have to get that cuckoo to sing to you from the south; "Cuckoo from the south will button up your mouth!"' he chuckled.

'That's enough of your cheek!' said Mrs Pepperpot, 'kindly get me down to earth at once!'

It was not a minute too soon. As her feet touched the ground she grew large again. She waved goodbye to the squirrel, picked up her basket and hurried to the shop.

When she came back she had bought her husband's favourite sausages and two pounds of macaroni, and for pudding she set to work making pancakes with bilberry jam. Then she laid the table with her good china and put a lighted candle in the middle.

'Hullo, hullo!' said Mr Pepperpot when he came in, 'Whose birthday?'

'Didn't you hear the cuckoo?' she asked anxiously.

'What cuckoo?' Mr Pepperpot looked puzzled.

'You mean to say you didn't hear it either from the north

or from the east?'

'Good lord, no,' said Mr Pepperpot. 'Much too busy with that mechanical digger; blasts your ear-drums, it does, all day!'

Just then they *both* heard the cuckoo, and this time it was right over their heads on the roof!

'That's the best luck of all!' cried Mrs Pepperpot, giving her husband a big kiss. 'Now we really can enjoy our feast!'

Midsummer Romance

In Norway at Midsummer the sun hardly sets at all, and at night the sky is almost as bright as during the day. So how do people get to sleep? If they're young and gay they don't bother; they stay up and dance round a bonfire on Midsummer Eve or go for long romantic walks in the woods till they can't keep their eyes open any longer, light or no light.

But Mrs Pepperpot's dancing days are over; this Midsummer Eve she decided to take a walk through the wood to visit Miss Flora Bundy, a spinster lady who lived by herself in a little cottage. Miss Flora was shy and timid and had hardly any friends to visit her, so Mrs Pepperpot thought she would cheer her up with some home-made cakes and a bottle of home-made wine.

'I feel like Little Red Riding Hood,' she thought, as she walked through the shadowy wood with her basket on her arm. 'I hope I don't meet that old wolf on the way.'

But she arrived at the cottage quite safely and knocked on the door. There was no answer. After she had knocked three times she tried the door and found it unlocked, so she went in.

'Are you there, Miss Flora?' she called.

Still silence. So she put her basket down in the hall and walked through the little sitting-room to the bedroom.

'No wolf in the bed, anyway!' she said, looking down at it. But what was that? Arranged across the pillow was a row of wild flowers – each of a different kind. Tears came into Mrs Pepperpot's eyes:

'Who would have believed it?' she said. 'Miss Flora collecting wild flowers to put under her pillow on Midsummer's Eve so that she will dream about the man she will marry. How very romantic!'

Then she looked again. There were only eight flowers; to make the dream come true, there should be nine different wild flowers.

'Of course!' she said. 'She's out looking for the ninth one.'

And, sure enough, when she looked through the window, there was Miss Flora walking up the path very slowly, her eyes fixed on the ground.

Mrs Pepperpot was just wondering how to explain her being in Miss Flora's bedroom, when she SHRANK!

Quick as lightning, she grabbed the edge of the sheet and climbed up, hand over hand, till she reached the pillow. Then she slipped in under it and lay still as a mouse.

Miss Flora came in and sat down on the chair by the window. As lonely people often do, she talked aloud to herself:

'It looks as if I won't find that ninth flower again this

year. Ah well, perhaps it's all for the best! It would be dreadful if I dreamed about anyone else but the dear postman!'

'The postman, eh?' muttered Mrs Pepperpot under the pillow, 'If anything, he's more shy than Miss Flora!'

'I'll just count the flowers once more,' said Miss Flora, when she had changed into her nightdress and was ready to get into bed.

Slowly she began to count: 'cornflower one, buttercup two, cowslip three, bluebell four, dandelion five, wild rose six, honeysuckle seven, poppy eight, cornflower nine.'

Did you notice? Miss Flora counted the cornflower twice. But *she* didn't notice that Mrs Pepperpot had put out her tiny hand from underneath the pillow and popped the cornflower from the beginning of the row to the other end!

Miss Flora clapped her hands and snatched up the flowers:

'There *are* nine. Hooray! Now I will go to sleep and dream about the man I love.' And she tucked the little posy under the pillow – right next to where Mrs Pepperpot was lying!

When Miss Flora had gone to sleep, Mrs Pepperpot eased herself from under the pillow and slid gently down the side of the bed on to the writing-table by the window.

As I told you, it was not really dark at all, so she quickly found a piece of paper and a pen. Being so small, she had some difficulty in holding the pen and writing the words large enough. But she managed it at last. Then she found a pink envelope and put the note inside. She wrote some more words across the front. Then she stood in the open window and gave a little whistle.

The sound was heard by a swallow in her nest under the eaves.

'I know who that is,' said the swallow, swooping down on to the window-sill. 'At your service, Mrs Pepperpot!'

'Thank you, Swallow,' said the little old woman, holding out the envelope. 'Will you please take this to the postman's house? But make sure he sees it, even if you have to wake him up with a peck on his nose!'

'No sooner said than done,' said the swallow and was gone.

Mrs Pepperpot sat on the window-sill, swinging her little legs and enjoying the warm night air. It wasn't long before the bird was back.

'Did you deliver the letter?' asked Mrs Pepperpot.

'Yes,' laughed the swallow. 'You should have seen the postman jump out of bed when I pecked his nose; he must have thought a wasp stung him!'

'But did he read what it said on the envelope?'

'He did. And I left him pulling on his trousers as he rushed out to get his bicycle. He should be on his way.'

'Good, good. My plot is working very well!' said Mrs Pepperpot, and thanked the swallow for her help.

The she sat down again to watch how things turned out.

But a postman on a bicycle takes much longer than a swallow on the wing to get from the village to the cottage in the wood, and Mrs Pepperpot was almost out of patience when he arrived, puffing a little from pedalling so hard. He was a tall, thin man who usually wore a sad expression on his face. This was because he was lonely and had no one to care for him at home.

Now, as he stood in front of the little cottage, Mrs Pepperpot could see he was smiling.

'At last!' he said, 'For years I've waited for this chance to visit dear Miss Flora. And now perhaps I can bring her good news this Midsummer morning.'

So Miss Flora had never had a letter delivered before? thought Mrs Pepperpot: 'The poor lady! Won't she be surprised?'

The postman went up to the door and gave first a timid knock, then a louder one. He was just about to knock for the third time, when the door opened, and there stood Miss Flora in a pretty flowered dressing gown.

'Oh!' she gasped. 'Is it really you, Postman?'

'I've brought you this letter,' he said, holding out the pink envelope.

'For me?' Mis Flora looked very surprised. 'Who can have written to me?' And she opened the letter then and there.

The postman waited while she read it: 'I hope it brings good news?'

'How strange,' she said. 'Just one line: "Congratulations and best wishes from the queen of the flowers".'

Peeping from behind a flower-pot on the window-sill, Mrs Pepperpot now saw the postman kneel on one knee in the dewy grass and heard him say:

'Dearest Miss Flora, to me *you* are the queen of the flowers!'

And what did Miss Flora do? She kissed her dear postman and they went indoors, hand in hand.

At the same moment, Mrs Pepperpot fell off the window-sill and grew to her normal size.

'Well,' she said to herself, as she walked home. 'That was a good Midsummer night's work. I hope they find the cakes and wine for their celebration.'

Mrs Pepperpot and the Pedlar

In August Mrs Pepperpot's garden was full of bright dahlias and asters and marigolds. They made her feel so cheerful, she decided to put on her new blue and yellow striped skirt with a clean white blouse, fastened at the neck with a red brooch.

From the oven came the delicious smell of a ginger cake she was baking, and she was just about to put on the coffee-pot, when a shadow passed across the window.

Before he had time to knock on the door, Mrs Pepperpot saw who it was. She rushed to the cupboard and pulled out an old black shawl and threw it round her shoulders. It hung well down over her striped skirt and when she had mussed up her hair and looked really miserable, she went to the door and opened it.

'Come in,' she said in a funny old granny voice, and in walked the person she least wanted to see that day, Mr Trick. A travelling salesman he called himself, but he was more like an old-fashioned pedlar, he had so many different things in his suitcase. He had the knack of calling just when Mrs Pepperpot had managed to save up a little money (which she kept in a cracked blue cup), and by the time he left she had always somehow spent every penny.

'Hullo, hullo, hullo!' he greeted her loudly. 'Are we doing a little business today?'

'How can a poor old woman like me do business?' she asked in that squeaky voice. 'Where would I get the money from?'

'Got it all safely stashed in the bank, I suppose,' laughed Mr Trick. 'Not like me, never make enough to put in the bank. All I get from some people are kisses and promises.'

Mrs Pepperpot had to laugh at his cheek, and soon there she was, rummaging through his open suitcase and pick-

ing out useless things like cotton ribbon and a coffee strainer, though she had two already. Meanwhile Mr Trick went on talking about banks:

'No, I don't believe in them; make it a point of honour never to have a bank book.'

'*I* make it a point of honour never to burn a cake,' said Mrs Pepperpot. 'So I'd better go and see if it's done.'

'Allow me, Mrs Pepperpot,' said Mr Trick, 'I'm an expert on baking. I will inspect your cake while you go on inspecting my goods.' And he went out into the kitchen.

Mrs Pepperpot went on rummaging, and at the back of the suitcase she found a secret pocket. There was a book in it, and when she pulled it out she saw it was a bank book with Mr Trick's name inside!

'No bank book, indeed! I'll teach you a lesson, Mr Smart Alec Trick.' And she hid the book behind the curtain. But when she turned back to the suitcase, she SHRANK and tumbled in among the hankies, socks and other fancy goods.

When Mr Trick came back he was surprised not to find her and called out her name a couple of times. But then he closed the suitcase and seemed in a hurry to leave. He strapped it on the back of his moped, and soon poor Mrs Pepperpot was having a very bumpy ride along the main road to the next town. There Mr Trick took the suitcase with him into the biggest bank and opened it on the counter.

Luckily he was talking to the cashier when Mrs Pepper-

pot sneaked out of the case and hid behind some forms on the counter. Because now he started looking for that bank book and had everything out of the case in his frantic search.

'What can I have done with it?' he wailed. 'I want to pay in some more money, and I'm sure I put the bank book in my case when I left home.'

The cashier told him he could just sign a piece of paper to show how much he was paying in, and Mr Trick pulled out lots and lots of notes from his inner pocket. Last of all he counted out some small coins; they came to exactly the amount that Mrs Pepperpot had saved in the cracked blue cup at home!

'Well!' said Mrs Pepperpot to herself. 'You not only tell

lies, but steal a poor woman's savings! If I was my right size I'd call the police.'

But she was still tiny, so what could she do? She puzzled for a moment, then she hit on an idea. Pulling out one of the forms from its holder, she dipped her finger in the ink-stand and wrote as large as she could:

'Your bank book has been found at Mrs Pepperpot's. Please fetch it at once.'

She pushed the piece of paper along the counter, so that Mr Trick would see it when he stopped chatting to the cashier.

'What an extraordinary thing!' said Mr Trick when he read it. 'Someone must have telephoned.'

While he and the cashier were trying to work this out, Mrs Pepperpot slipped back in the suitcase and was relieved when it was picked up and strapped onto the moped again. Off they went on the bumpy road back to Mrs Pepperpot's house. When they got there Mr Trick rushed straight to the door. As he knocked, there was the most terrific bang! He looked back and there stood Mrs Pepperpot, as large as life, beside his moped with the contents of his suitcase strewn all over the hillside!

'D'you keep bombs in your case?' she asked innocently, as she came forward to open the door.

'Certainly not!' said Mr Trick, who looked very un-comfortable. 'I had a message about a book I had left. . . .'

'A *bank* book, Mr Trick,' said Mrs Pepperpot, 'with your name clearly on the inside.'

'Well, yes . . . .' he answered, 'of course, it was my little joke about not using banks. . . .'

'Your joke, too, I suppose, to take a poor old woman's savings from a cracked blue cup?' And she went over and turned the cup upside down. It was empty.

'I can explain – honestly I can!' Mr Trick was talking very fast now; 'I took the cake out of the oven and put it on the table. Then I saw the money and was bringing it in for you to pay me for the goods you chose and then you'd disappeared!'

'A likely story! I ought to call the police and show you up for the menace you are to poor old women like me. Now give me my money and be off before I change my mind.'

With a trembling hand, Mr Trick counted out the money he had stolen and was just about to slink off, when Mrs Pepperpot called him back.

'You've forgotten something,' she said and handed him his bank book.

The Moose Hunt

There's one week in the year that Mrs Pepperpot hates: that's the first week in October when people with guns are allowed to shoot the moose. All the rest of the year the big animals roam in the forest as they like and nobody hurts them.

Mrs Pepperpot had her special friend, the big bull moose, and in the summer she was always running down to the stream at the edge of the forest with cabbage leaves or lettuce for him. In winter during the snow she put down great armfuls of hay. So neither the big bull moose nor his friends and relations ran away when they saw her coming.

But as the time came near for the shooting to begin, Mrs Pepperpot got more and more agitated. How could she warn the moose not to come out in the open, but to stay hidden deep in the forest?

Several days before the hunt she stopped taking green stuff down to the place where she usually fed them. Instead she took a dustbin lid and a wooden ladle and stood there, banging away and shouting as loud as she could to frighten the animals away.

Then came the night before the hunt and Mrs Pepperpot was walking up and down in her sitting-room, wringing her hands.

Mr Pepperpot took no notice; he was very proud of the fact that he had been asked to take part in the hunt with two local big-wigs, Mr Rich, the landowner, and Mr Packer, the chain-store grocer. They would be coming to fetch him early in the morning, and Mr Pepperpot was busy getting his green felt hat and jacket ready.

'How can you be so heartless and cruel?' asked Mrs Pepperpot tearfully.

'Nonsense, wife,' he answered. 'The hunt only goes on for ten days and only a few moose get shot. After all, we can't have those great elephants tramping down all the young trees, can we? Besides, it's good sport.' And he took down his gun to give it a clean.

'They're not elephants; they're very graceful,' said Mrs Pepperpot, 'and I don't want you to kill them.'

'Well, you can't stop me,' said her husband firmly.

'We'll see about that!' she muttered and walked out into the night.

She walked quickly down the hill, but just as she had crossed the stream and gone through the gate, she SHRANK!

'For once I'm not sorry to be small!' she said, picking herself up and looking round. 'At least the animals can understand what I say now – if I can *find* any animals.'

She started calling: 'Any moose about? Mooooose! Can you hear me?'

But it was so dark and her voice was so small and thin that no moose either saw or heard her.

But one creature did; her faithful friend, the squirrel. He happened to be sitting in the tree above her.

'What are you yelling for?' he asked and scuttled down the tree.

'Oh squirrel, thank goodness you've come,' said Mrs Pepperpot. 'You must help me warn the moose. They musn't come out in the open, for tomorrow the men will be there with their guns and will shoot them.'

'Right,' said the squirrel, 'I'll get my bush telegraph into action and send messages to as many as I can.'

'Thank you!' said Mrs Pepperpot, 'I knew you would help. But there's more to be done; I have a plan to foil those evil huntsmen. Bend down and I'll whisper it to you.'

The two of them whispered together for a long time before Mrs Pepperpot grew large again and the squirrel scuttled away to carry out the plan.

Mrs Pepperpot went home; now she could sleep with a quiet mind. In the morning her husband thought she must have come to her senses at last, for there she was on the doorstep with him, ready to greet the smart hunters with their picnic baskets and expensive guns and dogs.

Mrs Pepperpot was a little surprised to see Mrs Rich there as well, all dressed up in check trousers and a big feather in her hat. But she smiled at her too, and wished them all a good day's hunting as they left.

Then Mrs Pepperpot went shopping. On her way down she met Nora North, who said:

'Fancy seeing you out today. I thought you'd be sitting at home crying your eyes out for the poor moose.'

Mrs Pepperpot put on a solemn face and answered: 'Yes, it's a sad day for me and all animal lovers. But there we are, I can't change the law, so what's the good of moping?'

In the shop Mrs Pepperpot went to the counter selling toilet goods and First Aid things. She bought a good length of bandage, some splints and plenty of soothing ointment and witchhazel. The sales lady asked if Mr Pepperpot had had an accident.

'Oh, no,' said Mrs Pepperpot, 'but it's just as well to be prepared.' Then she went home again and waited.

Bang! A distant shot rang out.

'Oh dear!' said Mrs Pepperpot, covering her ears with her hands, 'I hope that was a miss.'

She went outside and stared anxiously in the direction of the forest. Wasn't that someone coming out of the gate? It *was*, followed by a sad-looking dog.

Mrs Pepperpot waited while the person slowly climbed the hill. When he got nearer she could see it was Mr Packer, but he was limping and supporting himself on a stick!

'Why, whatever happened to you, Mr Packer?' she cried.

'Oh, it was terrible!' moaned Mr Packer. 'My dog here had just got a good scent and I was ready with my gun as soon as a moose came in sight, when a whole flock of grouse came whirring out of the undergrowth and flew right at me! They knocked my hat and my glasses off and I ran into a fallen tree, giving myself the most awful bump. I'm sure my leg is broken!'

'Poor Mr Packer!' said Mrs Pepperpot, helping him indoors. 'Let's have a look at your leg.'

It turned out not to be broken, but Mrs Pepperpot put the splints on all the same and bandaged it so tightly, the poor man could hardly move.

Next to arrive was Mr Rich. You never saw such a sight! Not just his hat was green now; he was covered in grassy green slush from head to foot.

His dog had picked up a good scent which led them along the edge of a small bog in a glade. When suddenly a squirrel leaped clean out of the top of a tree on to Mr Rich's head, causing him to lose his balance and topple into the bog.

'I might have been drowned!' he wailed, squelching through the front door into the kitchen. There, curiously enough, Mrs Pepperpot had a big tub of hot water waiting, complete with a towel and dry underwear for just such an emergency. But Mr Rich was too wet and miserable to ask any questions.

'I hope nothing has happened to Mrs Rich and my husband,' said Mrs Pepperpot, looking quite concerned. They didn't have long to wait before the two of them came up the hill, holding hands and groping their way, as if they were blind. Which they were, almost. For they had walked into a swarm of bees and their faces were quite swollen with stings.

'Oh, you poor, poor things!' cried Mrs Pepperpot, 'how lucky I have some witchhazel!' And she set to work dabbing their faces and making hot cups of coffee for everyone.

'Blest if I even heard those bees coming!' grumbled Mr Pepperpot, when the rest of the party had gone home.

'God's creatures work in mysterious way,' smiled Mrs Pepperpot, 'and I don't mean only the human kind!'